Sweet S█

Longarm took the stairs tw█
empty, cane-bottomed chair still sitting ou██████
as soon as he turned into the hallway. With the Frontier
model Colt in hand, he slipped up to the partially open
door. From inside he heard, "Come on in, Marshal Long.
It's safe."

He stepped into the room to find Ardella Lasher, hands
raised in surrender, sitting in a chair she'd dragged in
from the balcony. Her double-holstered pistol rig, backup
gun, and bowie knife all dangled from the knobbed post
at the foot of the bed. She had unbuttoned her brocade
vest, removed the cowboy cuffs, and kicked off her fancy
stitched boots.

"I'm not armed, Marshal. Hope you don't mind, but
it's a mite more comfortable in here. Nicer chairs," she
said, then flashed a saucy grin.

DON'T MISS THESE
ALL-ACTION WESTERN SERIES
FROM THE BERKLEY PUBLISHING GROUP

THE GUNSMITH by J. R. Roberts
Clint Adams was a legend among lawmen, outlaws, and ladies. They called him . . . the Gunsmith.

LONGARM by Tabor Evans
The popular long-running series about Deputy U.S. Marshal Custis Long—his life, his loves, his fight for justice.

SLOCUM by Jake Logan
Today's longest-running action Western. John Slocum rides a deadly trail of hot blood and cold steel.

BUSHWHACKERS by B. J. Lanagan
An action-packed series by the creators of Longarm! The rousing adventures of the most brutal gang of cutthroats ever assembled—Quantrill's Raiders.

DIAMONDBACK by Guy Brewer
Dex Yancey is Diamondback, a Southern gentleman turned con man when his brother cheats him out of the family fortune. Ladies love him. Gamblers hate him. But nobody pulls one over on Dex . . .

WILDGUN by Jack Hanson
The blazing adventures of mountain man Will Barlow—from the creators of Longarm!

TEXAS TRACKER by Tom Calhoun
J. T. Law: the most relentless—and dangerous—manhunter in all Texas. Where sheriffs and posses fail, he's the best man to bring in the most vicious outlaws—for a price.

TABOR EVANS

LONGARM

IN DEVILS RIVER

JOVE BOOKS, NEW YORK

THE BERKLEY PUBLISHING GROUP
Published by the Penguin Group
Penguin Group (USA) Inc.
375 Hudson Street, New York, New York 10014, USA
Penguin Group (Canada), 90 Eglinton Avenue East, Suite 700, Toronto, Ontario M4P 2Y3, Canada
(a division of Pearson Penguin Canada Inc.)
Penguin Books Ltd., 80 Strand, London WC2R 0RL, England
Penguin Group Ireland, 25 St. Stephen's Green, Dublin 2, Ireland (a division of Penguin Books Ltd.)
Penguin Group (Australia), 250 Camberwell Road, Camberwell, Victoria 3124, Australia
(a division of Pearson Australia Group Pty. Ltd.)
Penguin Books India Pvt. Ltd., 11 Community Centre, Panchsheel Park, New Delhi—110 017, India
Penguin Group (NZ), 67 Apollo Drive, Rosedale, North Shore 0632, New Zealand
(a division of Pearson New Zealand Ltd.)
Penguin Books (South Africa) (Pty.) Ltd., 24 Sturdee Avenue, Rosebank, Johannesburg 2196,
South Africa

Penguin Books Ltd., Registered Offices: 80 Strand, London WC2R 0RL, England

This is a work of fiction. Names, characters, places, and incidents either are the product of the author's imagination or are used fictitiously, and any resemblance to actual persons, living or dead, business establishments, events, or locales is entirely coincidental.

LONGARM IN DEVILS RIVER

A Jove Book / published by arrangement with the author

PRINTING HISTORY
Jove edition / December 2008

Copyright © 2008 by Penguin Group (USA) Inc.
Cover illustration by Miro Sinovcic.

ISBN: 978-0-515-14552-6

JOVE®
Jove Books are published by The Berkley Publishing Group,
a division of Penguin Group (USA) Inc.,
375 Hudson Street, New York, New York 10014.
JOVE® is a registered trademark of Penguin Group (USA) Inc.
The "J" design is a trademark belonging to Penguin Group (USA) Inc.

PRINTED IN THE UNITED STATES OF AMERICA

10 9 8 7 6 5 4 3 2 1

Chapter 1

Dolphus Lasher didn't know it, but Deputy U.S. Marshal Custis Long had been hot on his evil trail all the way from Saragosa to Fort Stockton. Now, after nigh on three days of having his aching behind pounded to shreds in the heat and dust of West Texas, Longarm needed a bath, a hot meal, and the company of a good woman. If memory served, he felt pretty sure he knew exactly where to get all three.

He drew his weary, run-out animal up in front of a neat, well-kept cottage on the eastern edge of the sleepy military town, climbed down, and wrapped the reins around a rough hitch rack standing in the street. The sign, proudly displayed in the only yard he'd seen in all of Fort Stockton that sported actual green grass, indicated that he'd found the residence of Marybeth Fleming: Seamstress, Dressmaker, and Tailor.

He pushed the gate of the white picket fence open and strode up the crushed-stone walkway to a freshly painted, inviting front porch. Swept his hat off and tapped on the frame of a front door painted a deep forest green.

A tempting swing, large enough to seat two or three people, dangled from the ceiling on one end of the porch

1

and swayed back and forth on a barely moving, over-heated breeze. Beneath the swing a large, fuzzy yellow dog lay in the sparse shade and flopped its ragged tail in friendly acknowledgment of a welcomed visitor.

After several seconds of no answer at the door, Longarm tapped again. Still no response. He pulled the screen open to give the door a good, heavy-knuckled rap on its thick sheet of glass. It was at that exact moment he noticed a small, handwritten note stuck to the inside of the beveled pane indicating that the lovely Marybeth Fleming was out of town and would not be back for at least a week.

"Shit," he mumbled, let the screen snap closed, then stuffed the hat back on and headed for the street.

A sliver of broiling-hot, orange-tinted sun sizzled low on the western horizon. He had hoped to spend the night with the redheaded wonder of a woman whose words to him when they'd parted last were, "Don't be a stranger, Custis. Wherever I am, all you have to do is find me. You'll always be welcome in my bed." The smile that accompanied that promise assured his return for seconds, thirds, and maybe even fourths.

Thoroughly disappointed, Longarm stomped back to his mount and urged the beast on into town where he pulled up in front of the Sunset Hotel's rough entrance. He stepped down from the long-legged gelding, relieved the sagging animal of his possibles bag, his bedroll, his rifle, and his shotgun, then stacked the whole caboodle in a pile on the boardwalk.

A rough-looking, dirty-faced urchin of no more than twelve or thirteen sat on the step just outside the hotel's open front door. A smoldering, hand-rolled cigarette dangled from the scamp's sneering lips.

"You wanna make a dollar, boy?" Longarm called out.

The kid eyeballed the tired lawdog like he'd just found

2

something gooey and stinky on the bottom of his worn-out boot. "What I gotta do? They is some things I won't do, you know. No matter the money, they's jes' some things I won't do."

"Well, this ought to be right up your alley, then," Long-arm said. "Just take my worn-to-a-frazzle hoss down to the stable yonder and see to it he gets put up for the night, rubbed down, fed, and properly watered. Think you can do that?"

The ragged waif cast a second insolent, squint-eyed, judgmental glance Longarm's direction, then took an-other puff off his smoke. A hazy, blue-gray ring hovered over his filthy, unshorn head when he said, "Hell, yes, I think I can. Question is whether I want to or not. Not sure I want to even move in this heat for no more'n a fuckin' dollar."

"Give you two and that's it." Longarm slid the coins from his vest pocket, held them up for the filthy rascal to see, and rubbed them together. The metallic clinking of easy money brought the kid to his feet.

"What's your name?" Longarm asked.

Without hesitation the unkempt scamp snapped, "Reggie Atwood."

Longarm thought the mean-mouthed rascal might just lie about his name, so he cocked an ear as though he hadn't heard correctly. "Say again."

"Reggie Atwood, goddammit. You fuckin' deaf or some-thin', mister? Swear to Christ, it's got to where I have to yell for mosta you old codgers. Here I am, a poor unfortu-nate child, alone in the world, and I'm constantly havin' to deal with idiots. 'Nuff to make a body wanna eat cow chips."

In spite of himself, Longarm admired the boy's arro-gant grit, but as the mouthy, miniature rogue reached for the easy loot, Longarm snatched it away, then with a tired

3

smile said, "Don't screw this up, Reggie. You do and I'll find you and take this two bucks outta your skinny little ass with my pistol belt. We understand each other?"

Atwood flicked the still-burning butt of his cigarette into the dusty street, spit, then picked a stray piece of tobacco off his lip and rubbed it onto his leg. He toed at the dirt, then said, "Yeah, yeah, yeah. I ain't gonna do you wrong, mister. Swear I won't."

"That's Deputy U.S. Marshal, Reggie. Deputy U.S. Marshal Custis Long. And I'll throw your bony behind in jail if you jerk me around. Be sharin' a bunk with somebody like One-Eyed Bucky Matoose, who likes boys. Get the picture?"

Of a sudden the kid's demeanor went through a dramatic change. "Oh, hell yes, Marshal Long, sir. Wouldn't think of messin' you around any a'tall. I'll see your horse is well taken care of. Yessiree, Bob, sir. Hell, I'll even sleep with the long-legged son of a bitch. Horse stall's a damned sight better'n the alley where I usually stay anyhow."

Longarm dropped the coins into the kid's filthy palm. "Good boy. Tell the hostler I'll be around early in the morning for 'im. You remember all that?"

"'Course I can remember all of it. I'm a hungry, homeless orphan, but I ain't fuckin' stupid."

Two hours later, bathed, shaved, and feeling much better, Longarm downed another glass of Maryland rye at the Bugle Call Saloon's rough bar. Subtle questioning of a variety of tipplers, itinerant gamblers, and run-of-the-mill drunks and layabouts had led him to believe that Dolphus Lasher had already vacated the marginally pleasant climes of Fort Stockton and headed east as fast as good horseflesh could run.

Some of the local rumor carriers held that the murderous skunk had headed for Fort Lancaster and then perhaps

4

south to Del Rio. Others speculated that something nefarious seemed to be afoot with the iniquitous gent, but no one Longarm questioned appeared willing to speculate exactly what Lasher's wicked plans might entail.

Longarm pushed his empty glass aside, nodded his thanks to the slick-pated drinkslinger behind the bar, and then made his way back out onto the near-deserted boardwalk. The man-killing heat of midday had finally relented somewhat, and the stroll back to the hotel held the possibility of being almost pleasant and invigorating. Daylight would come mighty early the following morning, and the bone-tired lawman needed a good night in a comfortable bed before another chap-flapping effort to run Lasher to ground.

Longarm might've looked years younger than any man his age, but the previous several days of punishment in the saddle had left him hobbling around like someone had stood over his bed with a shovel and beat the unmerciful hell out of him. Nothing like a thorough ass pounding to get you in touch with portions of your spine that you didn't know existed.

He stoked a nickel cheroot to life and ambled back along the boardwalk toward the hotel. As he stepped off the walkway between the Bugle Call Saloon and a busy café, Longarm heard the distinctive sound of a palm being forcefully applied to someone's face. The resounding *smack* was followed by a woman's yelp and pleadings to stop. Longarm halted in the dark near the saloon's corner and cocked an inquisitive ear toward the action in the inky alley.

"Please, Riley, don't hit me no more," he heard a woman beg. "No need to slap me like that."

Another ringing rap echoed up from the shadows as Longarm turned and took a stealthy step toward the action. After several seconds in the deeper gloom, his eyes adjusted to the point where he could see the distinct but featureless outlines of a man and a woman.

Taller by a head and a half, an aggressive, angry ruffian had the defenseless female by the throat, pinned against the wall. He was slapping the bejabberous hell out of her. Every time she opened her mouth to object, he brought another staggering rap across her cheek.

"Done tol' you, LaCinda, you don't be messin' with Riley Puckett, 'specially when it comes to his pocketbook. You're supposed to have your cute little twitchin' ass out on the street makin' money for me. Plenty a soldiers in town every night. S'posed to be a-spreadin' that stuff a yours around. Pull 'em back here in the dark. Give 'em a good suckin', or whatever. I doan care long as you make me some money."

Puckett smacked the girl again. Then, in the poorly lit, trash-littered lane, Longarm spotted the glistening blade of a well-honed bowie knife.

"Oh, God, please don't cut my face, Riley," the panicked girl pleaded. "Go on ahead and beat on me all you like, just don't cut me up. Swear 'fore Jesus, I'll do whatever you want, I promise. Please God, just don't cut me."

"That a fact? Well, think I just might have to mark you up a bit to make sure. What the . . . ?"

Like the vengeful fist of a guardian angel reaching down from the golden steps of Heaven's pearly gates, the barrel of Longarm's Frontier model Colt caught Riley Puckett just above the left eye when he turned toward the puzzling rustle and rush of air that approached from the darkness.

A strange squeaking sound popped out of Puckett's mouth as the surprised pimp went to liquid knees, limply flopped to one side, then rolled onto his back. Longarm stepped on the knife, then bent over and snatched it up with his free hand. After holstering his blood-spattered pistol, he patted the moaning woman beater down for more weapons.

Puckett mouthed something that came out sounding like, "Arrghel snoffin' baffle. Squiggle glop."

Longarm grinned, hauled the near-unconscious man to his feet, and pushed him up against the wall. He jammed the knife into the plank siding next to Puckett's head, then delivered two short, bruising uppercuts to the tender, fleshy area just below the grunting man's ribs. Puckett made an *oof*ing sound and went down like a gunnysack full of anvils. Longarm snatched him back to his feet again.

Barely able to breathe, the huffing pimp gasped, "Who the fuck are you, mister? And why're you doin' this?"

Longarm got right in the man's face. Puckett smelled of stale whiskey, puke, and an opium pipe.

"Just consider me the vengeful hand of all the men in the world who just can't abide one who'd beat a woman," Longarm growled. "And, oh, by the way, I'm also doin' this just for the sheer fuckin' fun of it. 'Fore I finish, figure I'll be laughin' like one a them water-headed loons people up north keep in their basements."

A roundhouse left delivered to the chin sent a handful of bloody teeth swirling into the thick night air. An overhand right crumpled Puckett's nose and dropped the man in his tracks like a poleaxed steer in a Chicago slaughterhouse.

Longarm spit on Puckett's inert body, toed the man in the gut, then turned to the girl. She'd cowered down behind a rubbish-filled barrel and now whimpered as Longarm pulled her erect.

"It's alright, Miss LaCinda. Come with me. He's not gonna hurt you or anyone else for some time to come."

"Please don't hit me." The trembling girl placed a hand against Longarm's chest and tried to push him away.

As gently as he could, Longarm urged the trembling girl toward the street, then said, "Don't worry, Miss LaCinda, you're safe with me. No one's gonna do you any more harm—not tonight, by God."

He led the frightened unfortunate to a pool of light beneath the nearest streetlamp. In the dim, flickering yellow glow he examined her face for bruises and cuts.

"Well," he said, "doesn't appear he did any permanent damage. Couple a days and whatever bruises he might have inflicted should be gone. But just to make sure, why don't you come with me. I've got a room in the Sunset. We'll give you a better look there."

The hotel's desk clerk cast a toothy, knowing smile as Longarm led his newly acquired responsibility through the empty lobby. In the much better light of his room, he reexamined the girl and for the first time realized how young and astonishingly beautiful she truly was. Her angular, finely chiseled face was highlighted by full, pouty lips and eyes a color of azure he'd never seen before. Altogether the mysterious Miss LaCinda proved an astonishingly beautiful young woman. Not the kind a man would normally expect to find in the clutches of a vicious pimp.

Sitting on the edge of the bed, Longarm used a cloth dampened in the room's washbasin to dab dried tears and grit off the girl's beautiful, delicate face. She batted the long lashes of her sapphire blue eyes and said, "You're most kind, good sir. I do appreciate such selfless consideration and attention. Such behavior proves rare to find in this wild and wicked place."

"You should think nothing of it, Miss LaCinda. Any man worth his salt would've done the same. Any gentleman of breeding and conscience should be horsewhipped if he doesn't respond to a defenseless woman's cries of distress."

8

To his surprise, the girl took the cloth from his hand, threw it across the room toward the washstand, then placed his hand on her more than ample breast. "Please, let me show you just how much I appreciate your efforts at being the Good Samaritan, sir."

"LaCinda, darlin', that won't be necessary." While Longarm mouthed the words and sounded sincere, his hand remained attached to the girl's melon-sized boob.

Smiling, and with tears still damp on her cheeks, she quickly unbuttoned her dress, stood, and shucked the garment like an unwanted second skin. The striking and totally naked body beneath the discarded outfit that pooled at LaCinda's feet had an instant effect on the open-mouthed lawman. In a deliberately provocative move, she hefted both breasts upward, swirled her pointed tongue around the hardened tip of each thumb-sized nipple in turn, then sucked herself into a near ecstatic frenzy.

Never one to pass up such a blatant offer, Longarm hopped to his feet and set to ripping his own clothing off. In short order he had hung his pistol belt on the headboard of the bed and cast his last stitch aside.

LaCinda's wide-eyed glance dropped to her savior's enormous prong. She let out a surprised, snorting giggle, then grabbed him in both hands. There was plenty left over. "My word, I've never seen one this big," she cooed. "'Course I've only been a workin' girl for a short time. But, good Lord above, I'm not sure just how to approach a man with such God-given gifts."

Longarm pulled LaCinda close. He could feel the sweaty warmth of her body against his. The steely crowbar of love between his legs rubbed against her sweaty belly. "Well, let me show you, darlin'," he said, then swept her up and laid her out on the bed.

With as much caution as a first-time lover, Longarm stretched out on the bed next to the trembling girl, then

9

rolled to one side and set to nibbling at a still-erect nipple she had only recently abandoned. In less than a minute, the beautiful LaCinda made the excited cooing and gurgling sounds of a woman on the verge of gushing orgasm.

Barely touching her near-molten skin, he traced a fiery line up one leg until he found the steaming damp juncture at the heart of her now heaving hips. With two fingers he dipped into her sticky cooch, then skillfully caressed the hardened nub of the pulsating love button at the crux of her being. His wet, twirling fingertip sent the girl into convulsions of pent-up, noisy ecstasy.

"Oh, God," she moaned. "I've never felt anything like that before. Boys don't know anything and most men are so clumsy. So brutal. What you're doing is . . . Oh my God. Sweet merciful Father."

As LaCinda's legs moved farther and farther apart to accommodate her skillful lover's insistent, penetrating efforts, Longarm rose to his knees, then slowly settled into the welcoming comfort afforded by her trembling, parted thighs. He started the ride at a snail's pace, then gradually put on the speed after several minutes of plumbing the depths of her inner being to see just how much she could withstand. All evidence indicated that the beautiful LaCinda could take everything he had to offer and perhaps some more. My God, there's just no substitute for the energetic abandonment typical of youth and inexperience, he thought to himself once they'd got going good.

At one point, about midway through their wickedly carnal festivities, LaCinda flung her arms around Longarm's sweaty neck, pulled herself up, and placed an open-mouthed kiss on his ravenous lips. Their tongues dueled for several minutes before she broke the rapacious lip-lock, then licked her way to his ear and drove him to near madness with a ploy that had the power to bring most men to immediate climax.

The girl's incendiary tongue-in-the-ear move simply ensured that the flint-headed war club inside her got more rigid than a hard-rock miner's drill bit. The sweet lunacy that engulfed the heaving pair as a result of her enthusiastic wickedness spurred Longarm to ever more concentrated attempts to satisfy the conflagration burning between the near-insatiable LaCinda's legs. At one point she mewled, purred, and then pawed at her steaming notch.

Like a pair of high-strung, fine-bred horses entered in a stakes race, they lengthened every powerful, muscular stroke for the stretch run. LaCinda's eyes rolled into the back of her head. The entire upper half of her body flushed and appeared on the verge of bursting into scorching flames. Even in a momentary state of near catatonic bliss, she had the wherewithal to refocus, grab Longarm around the neck with one hand, pull herself up, and crane her neck forward in order to watch the stirring action going on between their legs.

Longarm threw his head back and laughed out loud when she somehow managed to bring her hips up with a resounding, gushing *plop* that welded her steaming, squishy gash to his belly like she'd been glued there by a talented paper hanger. Muscles stretched to maximum tautness, he locked himself into the shuddering posture of total, draining climax until he could simply no longer maintain the rigid, muscle-twitching pose. Finally, spent and thoroughly exhausted, he rolled to one side and slept like a dead man.

A bit after noon the following day, Longarm stood on the narrow gauge rail line's loading platform with the striking LaCinda. He handed the pouting girl a one-way ticket to El Paso and twenty dollars in cash. They had spent all morning talking. He'd learned the truth of her short, sad history—that her name was actually Lou Ella Potts and

11

that a distraught family still anxiously waited in hope that she'd come to her senses and return to Roswell, New Mexico.

He placed an arm around the girl's narrow, youthful shoulders. "You're sure you're going straight back home, right darlin'?"

"Yes, Custis, I'm absolutely certain. You needn't worry. There's nothing holding me here. I left home to see the elephant. Thought I'd live something akin to the good life in the bright lights of the big city. Used to pass by Roswell's night spots when we'd visit town on Saturdays. All colorful lights, music, and beautiful people. Well, that lasted about one day for me. Riley had me in tow so fast my head's still spinning. I've wanted to go back home for weeks, but just didn't have the means or the power to get away from him."

When the steam-belching, westbound train finally pulled up, Longarm kissed a red-eyed Lou Ella Potts on the forehead. "Don't you fail me now. Get on back home like we agreed. Find yourself a good man. Girl who looks like you won't have any trouble in that area a'tall. Get yourself married. Have a houseful a kids. Live a decent life and forget about what went on here. Promise me that."

She went on tiptoe and kissed his waiting cheek. "As God is my witness," she whispered, then disappeared into the billowing cloud of steam that floated back along the tracks from the narrow gauge line's belching Baldwin engine. And just like that, she was gone. And just like that, Longarm turned on his heel and didn't look back.

He snatched his animal's reins from the hitch rail and with the same hand grabbed the horn on the saddle. Before he could get his foot to the waiting stirrup, a stunning blow to his upper back knocked Longarm's hat off and dropped him to the ground like a sack of rocks. Stunned, he rolled to one shoulder and gazed up at a snaggle-toothed, grinning Riley Puckett. Wild eyed and drooling, Puckett's tongue darted here and there between his remaining teeth. Bloodshot, blackened eyes blazed with uncontrolled hatred. The big end of a shortened pool cue rested on one shoulder.

"Stupid son of a bitch. You actually think I'd let a beatin' like the one you gave me just pass with not even so much as a by your leave?" He swung the stout club again and sent a bolt of flaming pain from Longarm's elbow up to his shoulder.

The realization of what was about to occur darted across the backs of the downed lawman's eyes. He spun around on his side, kicked out one leg, caught his assailant behind the knees, and brought Puckett to the ground in a huffing heap. With a speed that belied his size, the red-faced, stringy-muscled lawman rolled on top of the crazed pimp and pinned him down. The grappling tussle rolled both men beneath the skittish horse. A well-shoed hoof dropped on Puckett's hand and set the man to squealing like a stuck porker. The pool cue rolled from his hand.

With the lapel of Puckett's jacket firmly in hand, Longarm struggled to his knees, then staggered to his feet. He snatched the now-mewling, begging pimp to a standing position, then brought a thunderous uppercut all the way from the ground. The bone-crunching blow caught Puckett below the tip of his chin. Several more teeth squirted from the man's mouth when his jaws crashed together. A second blow landed right between the surprised ambusher's eyes. With all the grace of a bison shot with a Sharps Big .50, the cross-eyed, unconscious pimp went as limp as a wet bar rag, then went down like a cannonball dropped in the ocean.

On unsteady legs, Longarm stumbled over to his snuff

brown Stetson, grabbed it up, slapped it against his thigh, then stuffed it back on his head. He wobbled over to the skittish horse, fumbled around till he grabbed the reins, then pulled the horse closer and patted the animal on the neck.

"Steady now, steady. Nothin' to be afraid of," he said.

After he'd clumsily climbed aboard his dancing mount, Longarm gazed into the floating cloud of steam left by the departing locomotive and wondered how things would have turned out if a hot and willing Marybeth Fleming had been in town. A quizzical expression of pained regret spread across his tanned, handsome face. He shook his head, bent over, heaved a gob of gooey phlegm from the back of his throat, and spit on the barely moving chest of Riley Puckett. Then he spurred the rested and ready hay burner into the vast emptiness of South Texas.

Chapter 2

Tired, bruised, dust-covered, and crankier than a red-eyed cow, Custis Long reined his lathered mount up next to the broken plank sign nailed to a gnarled, lightning-struck hackberry tree. He arched his back, twisted in the saddle, then massaged his elbow where Riley Puckett had smacked him with the pool cue. Jagged letters burned into the sun-bleached marker declared the jerkwater settlement ahead as Devils River, Texas, population 347— not including dogs, cats, pigs, or Mexicans.

The river, what there was of it, leaked by in an ankle-deep stream that a crippled frog could have jumped. The town appeared to run about a hundred yards east and west, like a well-aimed pistol shot, along a natural bend in the torpid stream's languorous march to join up with the Rio Grande some sixty miles to the south. As was the case with many of West Texas's tiny, barely existent settlements, Devils River's dusty central thoroughfare resembled that of an early Kansas cattle town and appeared to have no other streets crossing it. Even so, an impressive number of freestanding frame houses, adobe shacks, and even some tents dotted the landscape behind the town's run-down collection of false-fronted buildings.

Longarm snatched off his hat, slapped what filth he could from grimy arms, legs, and chest, then ran gritty fingers through sweat-drenched hair. With his hat hanging from the thin, rigid horn of his rented California-style saddle, he sloshed the last few drops of tepid water from a near-empty canteen over his parboiled noggin, then massaged the life-giving liquid into an aching, sun-baked scalp.

Twenty feet overhead, the hackberry's parched leaves rustled on a steamy breeze blowing straight out of the desiccated south. The whispering foliage offered some shade and a bit of relief from the cruel, punishing heat— some, but not very much.

A quick, slit-eyed glance along the peckerwood-sized burg's central thoroughfare gave the undeniable impression of a one-horse village teetering on the verge of being blown away. The abrasive, sand-filled winds coursing up from Mexico were blisteringly hot and dry enough to wither a rotten fence post.

Devils River's faded, sand-burnished storefronts— once gaudy, fancy-painted facades—and tired clapboard buildings slumped beneath the assault of a sun the size of a man's fist and the color of case-hardened steel. The only trees in evidence dotted the grassless yards of the dog-run houses, shacks, and flimsy tents that cropped up here and there north and south of the main business district like lost chickens looking for their coop. The physical situation of the rustic burg presented an observant visitor with the impression of a town sitting atop the only truly flattened area in the rugged, rocky landscape for miles around.

So far as Longarm could tell, very little or no foot traffic frequented the virtually empty street ahead. Here and there, though, drowsy hay burners stood at the hitch rails and sagged under heaven's oppressive, blistering orb.

A drowsing Mexican sat on the boardwalk in front of a liquor store and napped beside a wheeled cart that sported a rough, hand-painted sign for Emilio's Tacos. Here and there, in any available shade along either side of the rutted, hard-baked street, other sombrero-covered heads bobbled in sweaty slumber.

Nigh on seven brutal days in the saddle in a bone-rattling, ass burner of a chase had come damned close to wearing the stalwart long arm of the law right down to the proverbial nub. The punishing pursuit had started in Fort Stockton, headed into the rolling, grassless nothingness of West Texas all the way to Fort Lancaster, then made a nonstop beeline south along the crumbling banks of an ankle-deep, slow-moving, scum-covered Pecos River.

Longarm leaned forward in the saddle again, rubbed his aching spine, then stuffed the snuff brown Stetson back on his still-sopping head. He leisurely pulled a square-cut, rum-soaked nickel cheroot from his shirt pocket and took his time stoking the stogie to fiery life. The liquor-saturated smoke quickly streaked its way to expectant lungs.

With a gentle application of the spur, the weary, blaze-faced blue roan between Longarm's tired legs ambled back into the scorching, remorseless sunlight and headed for the nearest business that squatted at the extreme western edge of the drowsing village. Tiny, drifting clouds of powdery topsoil puffed up in wispy clouds and billowed around the tired gelding's feet like a gathering storm.

A town's blacksmith and stable operation was, almost without fail, Longarm's first contact with local citizenry during any of Billy Vail's assigned raids. The double door to the Devils River outfit stood open, but no one appeared to greet him when he wearily stepped down from his exhausted animal. The tired lawman felt as though every muscle in his stringy, six-foot, four-inch frame had been tied in a doubled-up knot and then twisted to maximum tautness.

"Jesus," he mumbled to no one in particular, then bent at the waist and tried to stretch some of the kinks out of his cramping legs and aching ass. A crackling backbone snapped into place like the links in a trace chain when he came erect again. He patted the horse on the neck and said, "Don't know 'bout you, but I'm just about weary 'nuff to sleep on a roll a barbed wire, ole hoss. Bet you are as well."

He led the droopy broomtail to a half-filled water trough and then loosened the saturated cinch strap while the parched cayuse quenched its thirst. Once he'd made the trembling beast more comfortable, it stood hipshot, slurping up the tepid but refreshing liquid.

"Help you, mister?"

The request snapped Longarm's head up. He gazed over the hand-tooled saddle's still-damp seat at the most beautiful woman he'd ever seen strapped into a greasy leather smithy's apron. Nearly six feet tall, the rangy gal sported an astonishing shock of shoulder-length, ebony-colored hair and a lean, long-muscled shape that had the undeniable power to render most men into a state of mumbling stupidity and foot-shuffling insensibility.

Near as the more than interested lawdog could tell, there appeared to be a lot of woman socked into a pair of man's sailcloth work pants and a ragged, skintight, sleeveless shirt. The tattered cotton garment was stretched so taut he wondered at the flimsy, overtaxed piece of clothing's ability to withstand the stresses from a set of fandam-tastic, flint-nippled knockers. Appeared to Longarm as how the only thing that kept those melon-sized puppies inside her tattered, open-throated shirt was the worn leather thong that held the horseshoeing apron up.

With a chunk of rag that looked almost as filthy as the bib of her smithy's apron, the astonishing female dabbed

18

at a river of sweat dripping from the end of a perfectly shaped button of a nose. Then she did the same to a tiny rivulet that sluiced into the ample cleavage revealed by her skimpy shirt. She glanced up and caught him gazing at her ample bosom. One corner of her full-lipped mouth crinkled up into a half smile.

Jesus, Longarm thought once he'd managed to tear his glance away from her upthrust breasts, *this gal's eyes are a color of brown that comes right nigh on to being gold.* He couldn't remember ever having *known* a woman with gold eyes and wondered at what it could possibly mean when those eyes got heavy-lidded with unbridled lust and turned into fiery lava with an uncontrollable need for nothing more than plenty of what he had to offer.

Longarm flashed his biggest, friendliest, toothiest smile, then purred, "Well, ma'am, need to put this here run-out jughead up for the night. Maybe even a bit longer. Want the ole boy well taken care of. He's been pushed mighty hard for nigh on a week."

A glistening sheen of sweat covered her muscular arms as she continued to pat at her neck and forehead with the rag. The movement jiggled the girl's near-unfettered breasts.

Gal knows exactly what she's doing, Longarm thought. He wondered how often she played her little game of *now you see 'em, now you don't* with some poor drooling man who'd never be given the slightest opportunity to nibble on those fine-looking jewels.

"Just for you, mister, goin' toll is twenty-five cents a day, or you can leave the fantail here for a dollar a week. Price includes hay, water, and some oats now'n again. Even brush 'im down for you a time or two. I take good care of the animals left in my charge. And since I'm the only option you've got, might as well go on ahead and bring 'im in outta the sun."

19

Longarm glanced up at the wind-blistered billboard over the stable's gaping door. "Sign says Harvey and Son. Take it Mr. Harvey must've had a daughter as well."

The ruby-lipped gal shook her leonine head. "Man who painted that notice for my dad got it right, as far as it goes. I inherited the place about a year ago and just haven't bothered to have it changed."

"Ah."

"'Sides, once I'd thought on it a mite, figured as how the sign would look kinda strange if it said Harvey and *Daughter's* Blacksmith and Stable. Or maybe Belinda Harvey's Blacksmith and Stable. Or anything with a woman's name on it—bein' as how shortsighted men can be, you know."

"Yes, ma'am. I know. Think you're absolutely right. But, still and all, a man just don't run across very many in the way a female blacksmiths. Leastways not many as look like you, anyhow. Know what I mean?"

The sweat-drenched girl squinted and flashed a half grin, half frown. Her tanned face flushed and the gold eyes sparkled. "Yeah, I've heard that. Think I've heard that exact thing from damned near every man who's ever set foot in this place since the day I took over for my father."

"Sorry, miss, I didn't . . ."

She waved his clumsy apology away. "Hadn't been for my worthless brother's drinkin' habits and distinct aversion to anything like productive work, guess I'd probably be slingin' drinks in some saloon over in Fort Worth's Hell's Half Acre right now. Maybe hustlin' cow chasers in one a them parlor houses. Doin' the cooch in a smoke-filled dance hall. You know, womanly things. But, as you can readily see, I *am* the blacksmith in Devils River—the one and only, as a matter of pure fact."

"Say you inherited this place a year ago, huh? Mind if I ask why you decided to take on such a responsibility?"

20

From behind a twisted smile, the Harvey woman growled. "Well, if you must know, I was seduced and betrayed by a no-account man who proved himself about as worthless as one boot."

Longarm let out an involuntary snort of admiration. "Well, ain't that just about the way for all of us," he said, then pulled the roan around and patted it on the neck again. He handed the reins over to the strikingly shaped female. Their fingers touched, ever so briefly, and even through all the sweat and grease he could detect the distinct aroma of musky, eager, willing female.

"Let's do that dollar deal, Miss Harvey. That'un works best for me 'cause, in truth, I'm not exactly sure how long I'll be in Devils River."

"Fine by me. Whatever butters your biscuits just suits me right down to the ground, mister."

"Now, am I correct in assuming that you are *the* Belinda Harvey mentioned earlier? Didn't make a mistake here, did I?" he asked.

"That's right. But most folks just call me Bell. Leastways them as don't manage to get on my uglier, more disagreeable fightin' side," the snippy girl replied. She shot Longarm a somewhat annoyed, squint-eyed look and, with no further comment, led his drag-assed animal into the dark, interior depths of the cooler stable.

Longarm followed. Once his eyes had reluctantly abandoned Bell Harvey's rolling, hard-muscled caboose and adjusted to the stable's inner gloom, he watched with considerable interest as the slim-hipped, big-breasted gal guided his tired gut twister to a clean, well-kept stall and began relieving the animal of its load.

"I'll take the bedroll, saddlebags, Winchester, and sawed-off with me," he offered.

Bell Harvey grunted, then, as easily as any man could have, she threw the entire rig over the top rail of the stall.

21

Longarm marveled at the stringy-muscled strength the girl displayed with such seeming ease.

"Go on ahead and get 'em," she said, then snatched up a pitchfork and proceeded to toss hay into the roan's rough feeder box. Longarm eyeballed the gorgeous ass crammed into the stretched-tight pants as she bent over and forked up a load. *Sweet Jesus,* he thought, *bet this girl could use that drippin' wooly booger a hers in ways that'd make a man want to slap his sainted, white-haired ole grandmama right in the face.*

Longarm loaded himself down with all his possibles, then glanced into the adjacent horse stall. Of a sudden, and with considerable reluctance, his sharply focused interest shifted from Bell Harvey's intriguing and wondrously shaped ass to the distinctive, shiny-coated paint horse that stood out like a sore thumb.

Saddlebags, bedroll, rain slicker, and rifle dropped into a pile at Longarm's feet. An anxious hand came up to the butt of the Frontier model Colt's pistol mounted cross-draw fashion on his left side. He tugged the hammer thong loose, lifted the pistol, and resettled it in a free-moving, easily accessible spot that would make the gun effortless to place in action. A cold, prickly sensation rode a wave of chicken flesh up his back. Suspicious, squint-eyed glances darted into every available corner where a man might hide. Dolphus Lasher was a murdering son of a bitch, and Longarm didn't intend to take any chances with the man.

22

Chapter 3

Longarm tapped on the grip of his pistol with a nervous finger. From beneath an arched eyebrow, he continued to study every possible nook or cranny that might provide a hiding place inside the stable, then he said, "You talk with the man belongin' to that pinto pony, miss?"

The striking Belinda Harvey propped her pitchfork against the wall, then went back to wiping grimy hands on the nasty piece of rag. "Yeah, I spoke with 'im. Came in a couple a hours ago lookin' to board his mount, same as you. Angry, disagreeable sort, if'n I've ever run across one. Kinda man you don't want to let get behind you, if my personal suspicions mean anything. Poor horse was lathered from withers to hocks. Just managed to get the poor creature cleaned up right before you rode in. What the hell's your interest in all this, mister?"

In spite of himself, Longarm smiled at the girl's bold, kiss-my-ass challenge. The prospect of a tussle with the woman was one he might seriously entertain, but at some later time.

"Young feller?" he said. "Dressed in black? Flat-brimmed hat? Double-holstered pistol rig? Wears 'em up high, butts first, Hickok gunfighter fashion? Lots of hammered silver conchos decoratin' the gun leather?"

"Maybe."

"Little bit of a mustache? Long sliver of a scar on his right cheek? Comes nigh on bleedin' into the eye? Some say as how it looks almost like he's been whacked across the face with a hatchet?"

Legs aggressively spread, Bell Harvey placed fists on her hips and squared off as though she'd been challenged to a round of two-man fisticuffs and wouldn't mind kicking Longarm's stringy ass one little bit.

"Could be," she snapped. "Like I said, what's it to you?"

"No need to go and start hoppin' 'round like a lizard on a hot griddle, Miss Harvey. Feller whose pony you have there murdered a federal judge over in Santa Fe 'bout a year ago. He's a wanted man. Wanted by God, the federal government, and my boss, U.S. Marshal Billy Vail. And you were right in your assessment, he's a dangerous bastard."

Bell Harvey took a hesitant step backward as though she'd stepped on a rattler the size of a man's leg hiding in the hay. Shook her head and said, "Do tell. You're sure 'bout that?"

"Dead man was as fine a gent as you'd ever want to meet name of Elias Creed. Feller who owns this pinto pony walked right into the federal courthouse in Santa Fe, New Mexico, and shot Judge Creed deader'n a busted singletree. Did the deed while the judge was presidin' over an unrelated case. Bold-as-brass killer's name is Dolphus Lasher."

The strutting Miss Harvey's demeanor changed, softened dramatically. Fisted hands dropped to her sides. For the first time she gazed at Longarm as though he weren't simply a nuisance to be dealt with as quickly as possible.

24

"Sweet forgivin' Jesus. This feller you're askin' 'bout any kin to the one and only Kermit Lasher?"

"One of that ole man's idiot sons. Not the oldest or meanest one, but he's one of 'em for certain sure."

"Hell's eternal fire, almost every livin' soul in this part of Tejas has heard of Kermit Lasher. Saw him once myself over in El Paso several years back. Men hung their heads and stepped aside, women blushed, and little kids cried when he stomped past. Hate to have that wretched-lookin', murderin' ole polecat after me."

"Well, I'm here for the son, not the father."

"Don't bear any resemblance to his father at all, if memory serves. But, you know, I just kinda had the feeling that feller looked and acted a mite on the dangerous side."

"Do tell."

"Absolutely. See, even as far back as the days when I worked here for my father, it's never been hard for me to spot his sort. Women and girls have to be careful 'round men of that ilk, you know. Even if you're just rentin' animals like them ole boys a stall for their horses. But, good Lord, I never figured the man for a cold-eyed killer."

"Well, the U.S. marshal in Denver, the redoubtable Mr. Billy Vail, wants young Dolphus gathered up and brought back to the federal lockup for suitable trial and hangin', if possible. Dead, if not. That's why I'm here."

"You a federal lawman?"

Longarm tipped his hat. "Custis Long, Deputy U.S. Marshal, at your humble service, Miss Harvey. Yep, young Dolphus went and grabbed the wrong dog by the tail when he killed a man of Judge Creed's importance. U.S. Marshals Service takes a damned dim view of such bold arrogance and downright stupidity."

The Harvey woman nodded and looked thoughtful. "Why'd he do it?"

"No one knows for certain sure. Gossip I've heard has it that Dolph went and got his balbriggans all bunched up in a knot because the judge sent one of his murderous, thievin' friends for a lifetime stretch in the federal prison up in Detroit. Seems the friend killed the hell out of an express guard durin' a train robbery."

"You don't say?"

"Well, there's other stories that try to explain the killin' in entirely different ways. Don't matter to me how you want to believe it happened. He's goin' back to Denver if there's any way possible to make it happen. Normally, if left up to me, I'd just shoot ole Dolphus's type and bury 'em, but Billy Vail wants this stripe-tailed skunk back alive, real bad. 'Course things don't always work out the way Billy wants 'em."

Bell shook her head and mumbled, "Lordy, Lordy."

Longarm snatched up his rifle and other possibles, then awkwardly touched the brim of his hat and did a slight bow. "Now, if you can point me toward a decent hotel, Miss Harvey, I'll drop my gear off and run the vicious little weasel to ground."

The eye-catching girl accompanied him outside and pointed to a sign about midway down the town's storefronted main thoroughfare on the north side of the street. "Davis House. Best digs in town. Feller name a Fred Davis owns the place. Just tell him I sent you his way, if he's workin' the desk. Ignore the joint on this side of the street—the Cattleman's. It's a real rat's nest. Wouldn't send my worst enemy to that place. Got bedbugs that can jump flat-footed from the chest of drawers to the back of your neck."

Longarm nodded his appreciation and started ambling toward the hotel. He'd barely taken two steps, when Bell Harvey called out, "Marshal, I know where your man is, if you're even the least bit interested."

Longarm stopped and cast an irritated gaze back at the girl. "Well, would sure help if you'd just go on and blurt it right out, Miss Harvey."

Jumpy as a man with a scorpion in his pants, she spit and then pawed the gob of phlegmy liquid into the thick layer of dust at her feet. "Saloon. Right next door to the Davis House actually. Place called the Matador. That Lasher feller's feet hadn't touched the ground good 'fore he started askin' as to where he could play some poker and get somethin' to drink. Don't frequent the place myself, but I've heard that the Matador's about as good a place as any. Much better'n the Ice House, or even the Rusty Pump 'cross the street next to the Cattleman's hotel."

Longarm threw a quick glance up the street past the Davis House, then turned back to Bell Harvey. "Appreciate it if you didn't mention our conversation to anyone till this whole dance shakes out. Would hate to walk in on the evil skunk after he'd found out I'm here."

"Oh, I understand, Marshal Long. Won't say a word. You can trust me."

"One other thing, Miss Harvey."

"Bell. Call me Bell, Marshal. Everyone else does."

"Well, Bell, what's your local lawman's name?"

"Quincy Bates. Town marshal. His office is a few doors down from the Matador, but on this side of the street. Wouldn't know it by what you can see now, but Devils River has a right fine jailhouse. Don't get used much though. Good place to lock that Lasher feller up, if you can keep from killin' 'im. And trust me, Quincy's gonna be mighty glad to see you."

"Why's that?"

"Aw, you know, I just figured as how since he's got a well-known, reputed killer runnin' around loose here in town, he'd be right pleased to have any help you might be able to throw his way."

Longarm nodded, took one last lip-licking look at Devils River's eye-catching blacksmith, then shook his head, adjusted his load, and turned for the heart of town. He hadn't gone far when, from behind him, he heard Bell Harvey call out, "Try Katy's Café for dinner later on. Few doors down from the Matador on this side of the street. Next to the marshal's office and jail actually. I take my breakfast and evenin' meals there most every day."

After a brief hesitation, and as though it were a hastily decided afterthought, she added, "I should be there tonight around seven."

Longarm stopped, turned, and cast a quick, interested glance back at the stunning woman. A leering grin, probably not expected to be seen, played across her face for about a second. Then she flushed up, abruptly turned on her booted heel, and hurried back inside the barn.

God Almighty, he thought, *that did seem a bit more than promising.* To no one who could hear it, he said, "Guess this shriveled-up ole town ain't quite as dead as it looks."

A self-satisfied smile etched its way onto Longarm's face as he trudged across the deeply rutted main thoroughfare to a rickety boardwalk, laid flat onto the ground. Didn't take much to notice that a goodly number of the storefront buildings along both sides of the street appeared to be vacant and boarded up.

The sad image of a town destined for wind-blown oblivion rapidly cemented itself when he noticed that several of the empty, forlorn buildings were former saloons or gambling establishments. Something must have gone terribly wrong for the pitiful burg of Devils River, Longarm thought. Even the most casual observer would've readily testified that it's a damned sad situation when you can't keep a saloon open in Texas.

Then again, he mused as he trudged along, the obvious

decline of Devils River could have been the result of nothing more than the primitive isolation of the place. It had been Longarm's experience that women liked the company of other women, and when such company proved scarce, or unavailable, they left for more sociable climes and usually took their men with them. Couldn't blame those lonely females much, as a sizable portion of Texas tended toward the big, the empty, and the painfully lonely. The forlorn, decomposing burg of Devils River appeared the crumbling model of such desperate desertion.

"Mighta been overly optimistic in my earlier assessment of this place," Longarm mumbled to himself.

Here and there he took note that sad, desperate-looking dogs had flopped themselves down in any available shady spot. One cur lay sprawled out next to an old man, dressed in the ragged garb of a former rebel cavalry officer. A once-jaunty yellow plume grew from the leather band of the old man's campaign hat.

The ancient soldier had whittled a good-sized pine picket into nothing more than a pile of curled wood shavings at his feet. His rack-ribbed mongrel flipped its hairless tail as Longarm passed, but refused to move off the boardwalk and out of the way.

By the time the tired lawman arrived just outside the Davis House's lobby, he'd worked up a considerable curiosity about Devils River, Texas, along with a powerful thirst, and he dripped sweat like a roasting pig on a spit. As he reached for the hotel's polished-brass doorknob, something totally inconsistent with his previous estimation of the town loomed into the corner of Longarm's eye and immediately drew his lawdog's probing curiosity.

A few doors down and across the street, hard by the marshal's office and jail, stood the imposing, redbrick Valverde State Bank. The only two-story building on the street, all observable windows on both floors were little more than fortress-like, narrow, shuttered slits and were covered with heavy bars. Near twice the size of any other structure on the street, the bank's massive oak doors faced the main thoroughfare and sported a set of iron gates that opened outward toward passing traffic on the boardwalk. Even more curious, right at its flat roofline, a series of barely detectable gun ports appeared to encircle the entire edifice. No horses stood at the hitch rack in front of the imposing structure and, as near as Longarm could detect, no people entered or left the place. *Odd,* he thought, *very odd,* then pushed his way into the hotel.

Chapter 4

As had been the case with the stable, no one appeared to greet Longarm when he strode into the lobby of the Davis House hotel. He dropped all his goods on the floor, banged the tinny-sounding bell atop the reception desk, then twirled the leather-bound register book around so he could sign in.

The thin, brassy tinkle of the bell still hung in the air when a rat-faced, popcorn fart of a fellow bustled through an open door located in the wall directly behind the desk. His straw-colored hair, carefully trimmed mustache, shovel-shaped beard of the same hue, and once-elegant but now frayed garments conveyed the image of a man who'd known a much better time, place, and station in life.

With an air of affected officiousness, the snooty clerk straightened his threadbare silk vest, ran a sweaty palm over pasted-down locks, then said, "Yes, yes, and what can I do for you, sir?"

Longarm continued to scratch his name and address into the hotel ledger. "Rent rooms, don't you?"

"Well, uh-uh-uh . . ." For several seconds the fussy clerk appeared totally disoriented by the question.

"Need a place to bed down for the night, and a bath if you can arrange one."

The flustered clerk waved a limp-wristed hand at a rack of wooden pegs attached to the wall behind his counter kingdom. Individual keys attached to numbered brass coins the size of a recently minted, gold double-eagle dangled from each and every one. "Well, by a stroke of pure luck, sir, the Davis House is completely, totally, and depressingly empty at the moment. You appear to be our only guest at present and can literally choose from whichever of our sterling establishment's well-furnished rooms you desire."

"Like a spot on the second floor, if possible. Prefer one with a window overlooking the street," Longarm said, and dropped the pen back into its ink-stained holder.

"Ah ha," the clerk knowingly snorted, as though he were a mind reader in a traveling carnival. "Number 201. Just the ticket. Most elegant accommodations we have to offer. Absolutely certain you'll just love it. Only room in our quaint, off-the-beaten-path hostelry that has a balcony furnished with a table and several very comfortable chairs. Grand spot to have an early morning breakfast, or watch one of our grand Texas days fade into evening." He clicked his heels together and flamboyantly handed the key over to his only customer as though it were made of solid gold.

Longarm glanced at the key, then said, "Sounds fine to me. Oh, are you Mr. Davis?"

"No, of course not," the snooty clerk snorted. "Mr. Davis is ill and won't be in for several days."

"I see. Well, send the bath up soon as you can, please."

"Might take a few minutes to rustle up the water for you, Mr. uh-uh-uh," the clerk mumbled, then twirled the register book around and glanced at the freshly penned name. "Mr. Long. Yes. Mr. Long it is, and of Denver, no less. My, oh my. You've come quite a distance to get to Devils River, Mr. Long. Well, hope you can forgive the delay, sir."

"Think nothing of it. Certain I've been dirtier and waited longer to clean up."

"Oh, if you're interested, there's a saloon right next door, Mr. Long. Fine, cool spot to seek respite from our punishing sun. You can enter through the café doors in the wall yonder. I would imagine that an ice-cold beer would taste mighty good on a day like today."

"Devils River, Texas, has cold beer?"

"Oh, yes. Yes indeed. Gent who runs the Matador has loads of ice brought in by special wagon twice a week from the plant down in Del Rio. He keeps that wonderful stuff in a thirty-foot-deep hole out back that's 'specially insulated with bales of hay to make it last as long as possible."

"Just be damned."

"Pipes the brew through a copper tube that's surrounded by the crushed ice. Quite a scientific undertaking, I dare say. Mighty fine drink on a hot afternoon. 'Least that's what I've heard. Personally don't imbibe myself, of course. Nasty habit, in my opinion."

"Damn," Longarm mumbled, glanced down at his pile of belongings, and then stared at the batwings. "A cold mug a beer sounds about as good as it gets right now. Even better'n a bath, to tell the God's truth. Hotter'n hell's front doorknob outside right now. Any chance you could have all my possibles taken up to the room?"

In a voice that came off like he was nigh on bored to distraction, the clerk moaned, "The staff of the Davis House lives to serve, sir. Be perfectly assured that your bags, baggage, and other accouterment will be in your room long before you finish your icy draught of liquid nectar."

Longarm grinned around a set of gritted teeth. He flipped a silver dollar onto the ledger book, turned, and strode to the entrance of the saloon on the opposite side of the lobby.

Before entering the Matador, the wary lawman placed one hand on top of the swinging doors and gazed directly across the room at the small but ornate bar situated against the far wall. Made of elaborately carved, highly polished mahogany and topped with a piece of slick, shiny black marble, the liquor-dispensing counter appeared, at most, only twenty feet long from one of its elegant ends to the other—probably a remnant of bygone and better days.

A sparkling glass case, filled with a variety of cigars, took up a sizable piece of the marble slab nearest the leaded window overlooking the street. The shriveled half of a sliced apple, for keeping the tobacco moist, sat in one corner of the case. Sign atop the glass container advertised a *good* smoke for five, ten, or twenty-five cents. For a second Longarm wondered what a twenty-five-cent cigar in Devils River, Texas, would taste like.

The Matador's fancy back bar sported four separate rows of bottles filled with a mouthwatering and colorful collection of enticing liquids. Most important, though, a tall, globular-shaped ivory spigot handle, in the very middle, proudly displayed the words Cold Beer in bold black letters. A gold-washed wire dice cage and a leather cup sat in a spot on the bar near the spigot where it was easily accessible for the bartender.

Longarm loosed the leather hammer thong from his cross-draw holster, then took one cautious step inside the batwing doors. Standing on the top of three steps that led down to the saloon's rough floor, he glanced from side to side. A combination faro layout and roulette wheel stood idle in the far corner on his right, along with the colorful board for a sucker's game called Hazard. Some Hazard operators used a tin dice-throwing horn for the game, which he knew was the origin for the derogatory term *tinhorn gambler*.

Four circular, green-felt tables, two on either side of the Davis House's private entryway, appeared fully capable of seating six to eight men comfortably at each. Saloon was virtually empty. Place was so quiet a man could easily hear his own hair grow. Behind the bar a banjo-shaped, schoolhouse clock ticked the day away.

The table closest to the Matador's set of batwings leading out to the main thoroughfare was the only one in use at the time. The black-garbed Dolphus Lasher had a seat in the game and appeared totally engrossed with his handful of pasteboards. A half-smoked hand-rolled cigarette dangled from the surly outlaw's curled lips. He'd picked a spot that put his back against the wall and was slouched down at an angle that gave him a fine view of the saloon's primary public entryway.

Three other brooding players smoked, thoughtfully squinted at their various hands, and pitched chips at a growing pot in the center of the table. The man Longarm had the best view of was obviously a professional—most likely the house dealer. He had stripped off his swallow-tailed coat, which now hung on the back of his chair, and rolled the sleeves of a spotless white shirt all the way to a set of fancy, scarlet garters cinched just above his elbows. In spite of those efforts to cool himself down a bit, the man's open, pasteboard shirt collar was clearly soaked with sweat.

As quietly as possible, Longarm slipped down the last two steps and eased across the open room to the bar. He placed a booted hoof on the brass foot rail, then took a fresh cheroot and fired it. An enormous polished mirror behind the back bar gave him a panoramic view of almost every nook and cranny in the entire room. And, more important, he'd picked a great spot to observe Dolphus Lasher without having to actually draw any attention by looking directly at the man.

Eyes shaded by a flat-brimmed, blue-bellied cavalry officer's hat, Lasher appeared not to have noticed the Matador's newest customer and single-mindedly studied his fistful of cards as though nothing else in the world existed.

As if by magic, a white-shirted, grinning drink slinger appeared behind the saloon's glistening bar and offered a friendly nod. Longarm slanted a glance to a spot in the corner next to the Matador's enormous front window that revealed a padded stool where the man had most likely been hiding.

The sweaty-faced bartender rubbed at a spot on the luminous black marble with a damp rag, then said, "And what can I do you for today, friend?"

Longarm flipped a finger toward the beer spigot and nodded. "Sure would like one a them cold 'uns. Gimme the biggest glass you've got."

The drink wrangler flashed a gap-toothed smile, then pulled from a rack beneath the dripping spout a clear glass mug that looked like it could hold a quart of liquid. He tilted the heavy container against the faucet's brass lip, carefully filled the thick-handled mug, then slid the froth-topped glass of icy liquid across the bar.

The amber-colored, spinning drink stopped when it touched the back of Longarm's hand. He snatched the frosty mug, pushed his hat back, and placed the cold glass against a throbbing temple, then rolled it back and forth. "Damn, that feels good, friend. Sun outside's like an auger tryin' to bore a hole in a man's head. Hotter'n a burning boot out there."

Bartender nodded, pointed, and said, "Yep, she's a

hott 'un fer damned sure. Go on, take a sip. Ain't nothin' like a cold beer to help a man through days like this 'un. Don't let 'er git warm on you, friend. Way too stifling an afternoon, so you'd best go on ahead and drink up."

The cold brew hit the back of Longarm's throat and slid down his dust-clogged gullet like golden ambrosia blessed by a heavenly chorus of winged angels. Mustache decorated with a foamy wreath, he eased the half-emptied mug back down, wiped his mouth on a gritty sleeve, then said, "Damn, don't get much better'n that."

"No, sir," the grinning bartender offered. "No, sir, it don't."

Longarm had barely raised the glass to his lips for a second stimulating helping of the soothing nectar of the gods when he heard, "Why, you four-flushin' son of a bitch. By God, I ain't got no use for card-bendin' bastards like you. Been a-cheatin' me ever since I sat down. Let me win the first few hands, then been second-dealin' on me ever since. 'Bout time you and me settled up on whatever your particular problem is."

A quick glance at the reflected action in the mirror revealed that Lasher had gotten up from the poker table and stood with one hand insolently hovering over the pistol hanging from a wide, double-row cartridge belt high on one bony hip. He loomed above the felt-covered table in a deliberately aggressive, wolflike stance. Squinted, rheumy eyes were locked on the nattily dressed gambler. The red-faced killer of innocent judges vibrated like a recently strummed human banjo string twisted so tight he just might snap.

As slowly as he could accomplish the move, Longarm grimaced as he reluctantly placed his sweating glass of cold brew on the bar and turned to face the festering disagreement. He cautiously flipped the tail of his jacket back, and then tapped the butt of his Colt with one finger. *Lasher pulls on this gambler, I'll likely have to kill him right here,* Longarm thought.

With a twitching gun hand suspended above his hip pistol's oiled walnut grips, Lasher leaned over and scraped the contents of a sizable pot into a rough pile on his side of the table. A string of slobber dribbled from the corner of his twisted mouth when he snarled, "Figure a feller that's on a first-name basis with the bottom of the deck won't object none, you stringy son of a bitch. Thought you could just pull the cheat on a stranger and then go on your way unnoticed, I s'pose. Otta jus' go on an' ventilate your guts right here and now."

Hands in the air, the gambler shook his head. A nervous spasm at the corner of the terrified man's mouth evidenced itself when he muttered, "I can assure you, sir, there has been no cheating here. You sat in on a square game. All you need do is ask the other gentlemen here at the table, or better yet, ask the bartender yonder. He knows I run a completely honest deck."

Lasher's flat, lifeless eyes blinked as though he'd been slapped. "You must think I'm some kinda fuggin' idget. Hell, I know your kind a dealer sure as I know every square inch of my completely nekkid body."

Situation got even more tense when a nervy leather pounder at the table pushed his seat back and attempted to stand. Lasher's pistol flashed from its holster. "Sit the fuck back down," the angry killer growled. "Move again, shit kicker, and I'll decorate the hitch rails out front a this thievin' joint with your innerds."

The flush-faced brush popper flopped back into his seat, raised his hands in supplication, then said, "Look, mister, I ain't got nothin' to do with no cheatin'. Been playin' poker in here twice a week for nigh on two years. Never knew anyone afore what claimed he'd been cheated."

"Well, you've heard it now," Lasher snapped. Of a sudden he glanced toward the bar. A nervous, fleeting look danced from Longarm to the bartender. "Get on over here, bar dog, an' gather up my winnin's whilst I keep an eye on this trio a back-stabbin' skunks. Sons a bitches who'd cheat a man'll shoot him in the back first chance they get."

The third man at the table—dressed in a three-piece, striped gray suit, white shirt, and tie—who looked like he might've been a local businessman of some sort, said, "Now hold on, mister. There's some of my money in that pile you're about to make off with, along with some of this hardworking cattle-wrangling gent's. You want to take the dealer's cash, that's just fine by me. But, by God, I won't stand for what amounts to highway robbery just because you think you *might* have been swindled."

Lasher stomped to the side of the table nearest the bar and made what Longarm felt was a serious error in judgment—he'd unwittingly managed to turn his back on the Matador's front entrance. He'd lost his temper and let his anger get ahead of a seething thinker box.

With a damp rag flipped over his shoulder, the Matador's booze slinger scuttled to the spot Lasher had just vacated, but appeared reluctant to do anything that even resembled scraping up the pile of money once he got there.

At about the same instant, Longarm's attention was drawn to movement at the batwings leading to the street. A quick glance revealed a tall, angular, clean-shaven, badge-wearing fellow who took a single, silent step inside, scanned the entire saloon, then hooked his thumbs over a webbed, military-style cartridge belt loaded with a row of shotgun shells and .45s. The town marshal's Colt was worn in a cross-draw holster strapped high on his left side. The unhooked hammer thong dangled to one side. Weapon and man appeared ready for instant use.

Unaware of his freshly arrived audience, Lasher skimmed his hat into the bartender's chest, growled, and shook his pistol at the nervous man. "Done tole you to pick my money up, mister. Now get at it. Jus' rake it all off the fuckin' table and into the hat. By God, ain't no second-dealin' buncha cardsharps from a no-dog, jerkwater town like this 'un gonna steal from me and get away with it."

In a voice that rumbled across the floor as though it came directly from a vengeful God hovering on high, the town's impressive-looking lawman thundered, "What the hell's goin' on here?"

Longarm's hand slipped to the grips of his pistol, but Lasher appeared to have been suddenly overcome by a flash of realization that he might have bitten off more than he could chew. He now had four men in front of him who disagreed with his assessment of the situation, and one behind. His hands went into the air as he turned toward the commanding voice. As soon as he fully realized just how big a hole he'd dug for himself, the arrogant scalawag got something akin to apologetic. He let the hammer down on his pistol and allowed it to dangle from one finger.

"Well, now," Lasher snorted, "no need for the fuckin' law to get involved in our little disagreement, Marshal. Think we can probably settle this difference amongst ourselves. Sort it all out and come to some kinda mutual agreement of how to make everything right."

The red-faced cowboy jumped to his feet again and yelped, "That's total by-God bullshit, Quincy. This son of a bitch accused Mr. Fauntroy here of cheatin' and was just before takin' all the money on the table. Stupid cocksucker was gonna walk off with mine, Fauntroy's, and Mr. Justice's as well. Man ain't no more'n an angry, no-talent thief far as I'm concerned. Think everyone a-playin' would agree with me."

Lasher grimaced as though tempted to gun the mouthy brush popper, but he slowly holstered his weapon, then growled, "Be fine with me if'n you could jus' let me outta here with what I came in carryin'. No need for anyone to get all upset 'bout our little difference of opinion. Truth is I've got more important fish to fry."

Fellow in the gray suit sneered. "Nobody else playing the game has any *difference of opinion* with the way it was being played, mister. Personally, I think you should throw this arrogant skunk in a jail cell for a day or two, Quincy. He's threatened everyone here and attempted robbery if nothing else. Few days in the Devils River *juzgado* should give him plenty of time to search around under his jailhouse bunk and maybe find some badly needed manners."

"Now wait a minute," Lasher said, "I ain't done nothin' what would warrant you lockin' me up. Them fellers can keep their money, jus' give me back what I threw into that last pot."

The gambler, Fauntroy, who'd dropped his hands and watched the proceedings with little in the way of comment, said, "That won't work, mister. You were losin' fair and square. Bald-faced truth is you have no talent for this game. Near as I can tell, when it comes to poker, you don't know your own ass from an outhouse door."

Lasher twisted at the waist and shook a knotty finger in Fauntroy's face. "Best watch your mouth, card bender. 'Bout one more word outta you and I'll be sorely tempted to put a powder-rimmed hole in your sorry hide."

While obviously uncomfortable with the situation, Fauntroy didn't back down. "Money on the table's gonna go to whoever was holdin' the best hand, but you ain't gettin' a penny of it. Not a single fuckin' penny, you thievin' bastard."

Lasher completely lost what little composure he might

have ever possessed. Snarling like a dog, he thoughtlessly twirled on the poker table and, at the same time, went for his gun again. His fingers had barely touched the weapon's grips when, in a blur of quick-thinking action, Marshal Quincy Bates took two long-legged steps and whacked the belligerent thug across the noggin with the barrel of his own pistol.

The stunning rap on the skull sounded like someone had dropped a watermelon on the floor. The pistol barrel opened up a slit above Lasher's ear as long as a grown man's hand. A spray of hair, skin, and blood filled the air and decorated the poker table like a gory rainstorm. Lasher's knees buckled, and he went to ground like a sack full of horseshoe nails.

Longarm couldn't help but smile as the three remaining gamblers hopped to their feet and immediately set to splitting up the money.

The bartender strode to Marshal Bates's side and patted the lawman on the shoulder as he holstered his weapon. "Sure glad you showed up when you did, Quincy. Was about to try and send for you when this jackass drew me into the disagreement."

Bates stepped over Lasher's limp body, snatched up the belligerent gunman's equalizer, and shoved it behind his cartridge belt. "Well, gotta get him down to the jail now. Might be a job, 'cause he's gonna be right limp for a spell, given how hard I hit 'im. Bet my bloody whack leaves one helluva messy lump on his rock-hard noggin."

"Be more'n glad to help you drag the evil skunk's sorry ass down to your hoosegow, Marshal Bates," Longarm offered. "That is if you can wait till I finish my cold beer."

Bates smiled. "Well, you go on ahead and enjoy your drink, mister. Hell, think I might just have one with you," he said and stepped over to the bar.

Longarm smiled. "Well, by God," he said, "it'll be my pleasure to buy you one, Marshal Bates. Man who can provide me with the best entertainment I've had in weeks deserves a free beer."

Quincy Bates grinned, then stepped up to the bar. Longarm slapped the man on the back and said, "Set 'im, barkeep. Any man who'll brace Dolphus Lasher deserves a drink."

Bates glanced back at the unconscious man, then said, "Sweet Jesus. Dolphus Lasher? You sure 'bout that, mister?"

"Yep. He's the reason I'm here. Fact is, you just whacked the idiot son of Kermit Lasher. Have a beer, friend."

Chapter 5

Custis Long and Marshal Quincy Bates downed a friendly brew together and ascertained that they liked each other. Bates, Longarm quickly determined, was one of those open, outgoing types who never met a stranger and could end up being a friend for life, if you just treated him right.

An hour later, Longarm slumped in an overstuffed, tack-decorated leather chair directly across from the battered, time-scarred desk of Devils River's gregarious marshal. The worn leather throne reminded him of the one in Billy Vail's Denver office. An unlit cheroot was clenched between his teeth. He flicked an appreciative glance around the well-appointed hoosegow, then pulled a fresh lucifer from his vest pocket, scratched it on the heel of his boot, and stoked the cigar to smoldering life.

As he snuffed the flaming match, Longarm continued to admire the neat, dust-free rack of well-oiled weapons directly behind Bates's chair. Next to the stand of rifles, shotguns, and pistols, an imposing wooden door with a small barred window at about eye level stood slightly ajar. The open entryway led to a block of four amazingly clean, well-kept cells. Made of thick timbers, the impressive gate to the iron-barred hoosegow was decorated with metal hinges and a sliding bolt as thick and substantial as the barrel on a Sharps rifle.

Dolphus Lasher wallowed in a pool of his own blood, spit, and other bodily fluids on the floor of the most distant of the cubicles. Bates had explained that he always put prisoners as far away from his desk as possible because he quickly grew tired of their endless bellyaching, complaining, and unreasonable demands.

A one-legged, grizzled old geezer of a deputy that Bates had offhandedly referred to as Hamp Bodine thumped around the cell block on his carved wooden leg. The gimp hobbled from one cell to another cell, pushing a ragged piece of straw broom, and constantly mumbled to himself as though carrying on a conversation with some unseen person.

In a raspy, toothless voice, Bodine called out, "He's done went an' puked 'gin, Quince. Sunuvabitch is makin' a helluva mess back here. You know how I hate cleanin' up after pukin' drunks. Jesus, it stinks like the dickens. Musta had some chili or somethin' fer breakfast, dammit."

Bates shook his head and rolled his eyes as though indicating to Longarm that his ancient deputy was something of a talkative mess and just had to be tolerated.

Longarm glanced away from the town marshal's smiling face and continued to scan the rest of the room. On the opposite side of the cell block's entry door, near a potbellied stove decorated with a well-used coffeepot, a neatly made cot was pushed into the corner. A number of framed, tintype photographs bedecked the wall at the head of the sturdy bed. A washstand equipped with an ivory-colored glass basin and matching ewer for water was strategically placed next to the head of the bed and directly beneath a nice-sized mirror hung from a wooden peg in the wall.

Here and there, in other corners around the room and

against the walls, Longarm noticed a number of wooden hat racks loaded with clothing, gun belts, and other such manly accouterment. A small, rugged table built from rough-cut lumber and three matching cane-bottomed chairs had a place just inside the front door. Atop the table, a faded, store-bought chessboard equipped with what appeared to be hand-carved pieces was set up and ready for instant use. Longarm marveled at the incongruity of that particular piece of gear.

Now and again, the split-scalped, sore-headed Lasher could be heard tossing about on the rough-timbered floor, moaning and then mumbling something unintelligible. Neither of the badge-wearing pair paid the slightest attention to the outlaw's semiconscious, incomprehensible ramblings.

Occasionally, Deputy Bodine wobbled up to the open doorway, glared at the two marshals, then grunted and disappeared again like a grumbling, discontented ghost. The local pill roller had been summoned and now there was little that either of them could do but sit and wait for the medicine man to show up.

Bates focused his undivided attention on Longarm's every word. Then, after several minutes of idle chatter, he pulled open a drawer of his desk and fished out an unlabeled bottle of locally bottled scamper juice along with three shot glasses. He filled two and pushed one over to his newly acquired amigo.

"You wanna have a drink with us, Stumpy?" he called over his shoulder.

From somewhere in the deeper recesses of the cell block Bodine shouted, "No, goddammit. You know I cain't drink that stuff this early in the day, Quincy. Makes my stomach hurt. Have to wait till after the sun goes down to do my drinkin'. Woulda liked a cold beer, though. Coulda brought me a beer, by God."

Bates grinned, tossed his drink back, slapped the glass down on his desk, shook his head like a wet dog, then said, "Whoa, mama. Hoogity, boogity. That's damned good stuff. Probably peel the paint off a New Hampshire barn door, but it hits the mark like nothin' else you can buy or make yourself."

Longarm saluted Devils River's lawdog with his dripping glass, then took a conservative but lingering sip. Although he grinned and smacked his lips, his eyes almost crossed. After a grimacing grunt, Longarm sputtered, "Pretty good for a bonded-in-the-barn bottle of bust head. 'Course, from the taste, I figure it wouldn't do to get any on my vest. Might eat a hole in it."

Both men laughed, then Bates said, "Feller who made this here beaker a pop skull's been at the trade for a long time. Brought his talents out to Devils River from Shelby County, Kentucky, a year of so after our little bump in the big cold and lonely was first established."

Longarm wet his tongue again with another nibbling hit on the glass, made a sound like a big dog growling, then grunted out, "When was that?"

"Right after Mr. Lincoln's War of Yankee Aggression. Ole Hamp lost his leg at Chickamagua, you know. Anyway, Devils River had mighty good prospects back then, Custis. Only town of any size between Fort Lancaster and Del Rio. Great place to rest up 'fore you continued your trip south. But, truth is, the town was and still is a bit off the beaten path."

"Surely have to be lookin' to find it, alright."

"Well, some local folks like to say we're halfway between wind-blown nothin' and Hell's smokin' front door. Ole Hamp says you cain't see Hell's front gate from the town limits, but just ride a few miles south and you'll find it."

"Ah."

48

"Look, Long, I'm certain you're just anxious as the dickens to get on back to the bright lights and all the hoo-hah of big-city Denver, but I have a somewhat selfish reason for hoping that you can stick around for at least a few days. I mean, shit, you've already got the low-life desperado you came after under lock and key, and I could use some of your grand pooh-bah of law enforcement kind of assistance just in case Lasher should get sparky and want to cause me any trouble."

Longarm took another sip of his drink, gritted his teeth, then said, "Right good-lookin' gal who stabled my horse said she knew for sure as how you'd just be happier'n a gopher in soft dirt to see me once you found out who I was after."

"Talkin' 'bout Bell Harvey?"

"That's the one."

Bates snatched his hat off, then threw it onto his desk and flashed a crooked, toothy grin. He ran sweaty fingers through his hair and gave his scalp a good scratching. "Gal's a looker, alright. Got more curves than a barrelful a West Texas rattlesnakes. Only female in town as I'm aware of what wears men's pants on a fairly regular basis. Best-lookin' woman in Devils River. Ain't no doubt about it. They's a couple a others what come mighty close, but she'd take the prize in any contest I had to judge. Least-ways, that's my humble opinion on the subject."

"Makes two of us, Quincy. 'Less my sight is beginnin' to fail me, Bell Harvey's got the face of an angel and the kind of figure that could raise steam off the icy heart of a man who's been dead for a week. Maybe even provide the poor departed with a nice stiff boner as well."

Bates laughed and slapped his knee. "That's a good 'un, Custis. Gonna have to remember that 'un. Raise steam off'n a dead man's heart. Boner on a dead man. Damn, now that's for sure 'nuff downright funny."

The sound of water being splashed onto the cell block's wooden floor snapped both men's attention toward Hamp Bodine's iron-bound kingdom. Bodine yelped, "Keep on a pukin', you sunuvabitch, an' I'll keep a-throwin' water on ya. Makin' a mess outta my jailhouse, goddammit."

Longarm pushed himself up in his leather-covered throne, then said, "Guess there's no great rush for me to get back to Denver, Quince. Suppose I could send a telegraph from your local office to Billy Vail and tell 'im I've been unavoidably detained for a few days. Wouldn't be the first time. He ain't gonna gripe, long as I can tell 'im I've got Lasher in tow. Besides, I need the rest."

"There you go. Now that's just the ticket. Be good to have another real lawman around until you can get the evil skunk outta town and back on his way to a well-deserved appointment with perdition."

"Tell the truth, Quince, I hadn't planned on heading back any sooner than tomorrow or the next day anyway. Need a real bath, a hot meal, and a night or two of restful sleep between some clean sheets. 'Sides, just might have to stick around and see if anything promisin' develops with the lovely Miss Harvey. Got the somewhat subtle impression she just might be a little bit more'n interested."

Bates threw his head back and let out a derisive grunt. "Well, good luck with that 'un. You be sure and let me know how it all turns out. Tragic tales of thwarted dreams and desires, real or imagined, do have the power to prick my twisted sense of humor. Always did get a kick outta watchin' another man crash against the rocky coast of female possibilities like a wooden boat and then fly into splintered pieces."

Longarm leaned forward and sat his glass on the edge of Bates's desk. "Well, now that's one helluva grim assessment of my prurient chances, Marshal Bates. Makes me all the more inquisitive 'bout the lovely Miss Harvey."

He flashed his most confident smile, then said, "Go on ahead and fill that glass up again, amigo."

Bates poured Longarm a second portion of Devils River's favorite homemade jig juice, then leaned back in his squeaky chair and steepled his fingers. "Well, whatever it takes to keep you around for a few days is fine by me. Guess you might've observed as how our little slice of West Tejas heaven ain't nothin' near what it used to be. As a consequence, I'm the only badge-toting type around for fifty miles in any direction—present company duly noted, of course."

Longarm took another gnawing sip from his glass before letting out a strangled cough, then saying, "Does appear that nigh on half the businesses along your main thoroughfare are closed up tighter'n a fat woman's stockings. Wondered 'bout that, but hell, West Texas towns do have a tendency to come and go. This 'un has all the earmarks of one that's goin'."

"Yeah, well, it weren't always like that, Custis. Ain't been more'n two years ago that Devils River was a thriving concern from one end of Main Street to the other. Looked like everything was movin' along 'bout as well as could have been expected, given the remoteness of our location and all. Have to admit the town ain't exactly along any of the most well-traveled paths a man could pick to go south, though."

Longarm squirmed back down into the comfort of his seat. "You can say that again. I've passed through most of this area more'n once and never stopped in Devils River for anything as I can recall."

"Well, anyway, two or three years ago we started havin' some problems with . . ."

Before Quincy Bates could get to his point, the jail's front door burst open and a short, intense, bespectacled man dressed in a frayed-at-the-cuffs, black three-piece suit, white shirt gone to a cream color, and string tie bustled in. The ever-present worn leather bag of a country sawbones dangled from one hand. He whipped a floppy, short-brimmed felt fedora off his dripping head and fanned a pinch-browed face with it. An odd silence followed the man as he stepped inside the room and quietly closed the jail's heavy door.

Chapter 6

The fidgety sawbones's sharp, inquisitive blue-eyed gaze darted from one lawman to the other. He nodded to each in turn before he focused on Bates and said, "Sorry I'm a bit late, Quincy."

"'S okay, Doc. No rush."

"Got here quick as I could. Had to make an emergency run out to the Sawyer place. Poor ole Brutus stepped the wrong way and fell out of the loft of his barn. Landed on a stall railing. Busted one arm up pretty bad. Compound fractures of both the bones in his lower arm. Prognosis doesn't look at all good for the man. Just hope he can get through the whole mess without getting infected. Splintered wing gets festers and I'll likely have to take it off."

Bates pushed his chair away from the desk, rose to his feet, then motioned toward Longarm. "Doc, this here's Deputy U.S. Marshal Custis Long. Custis, meet Sam Speaks, best pill roller I've ever known."

Speaks dropped his bag and hat onto one of the empty chairs sitting at the rough table topped with the chessboard. Longarm got to his feet and the men shook hands.

After the obligatory moment of awkward pleasantries,

Speaks turned back to Bates and said, "Hear tell as how you've got someone who needs some kind of medical attention back yonder in one of your cells."

"Yeah. Had to tap this ignorant slug on the noggin with my pistol barrel, Doc. Split his scalp open a little. He bled a mite, but I don't think I hurt him too bad. I'll go roust 'im out for you. Bring 'im in here where the light's a whole lot better. Mean-mouthed son of a bitch should be awake by now. Like I said, don't think I hit him all that hard."

Longarm watched as Speaks languidly strolled back over to the table and pushed the chess game, board and all, over to one corner. He placed his leather bag in the vacant space and snapped it open. Pulled out a glass vial of clear liquid, another that had a reddish yellow tint, several gruesome-looking metal instruments, a large sewing needle, and a spool of what appeared to be white cotton thread or maybe fine-drawn catgut. He pulled one chair away from the table and turned it so that whoever took a seat would best catch the light coming through the jail's unshaded front window.

Still dripping wet, bleeding, and drenched in blood, spittle, and crusted puke, a gaunt-faced Dolphus Lasher stumbled up to the cell block door. Man looked about one step away from bony-fingered death.

Quincy Bates shoved the dripping, rubber-legged killer forward and said, "Over there. Doc's gonna have a look at that little bitty cut on the side a your brain box." Town lawman leaned against the door frame and made no further effort to help his wounded prisoner negotiate the last few unsteady steps to the medical attention that awaited his still-oozing head wound.

Hamp Bodine hopped from peg leg to booted foot and stared from behind his boss like a small child watching something he wasn't supposed to see. He scratched his stubble-covered chin and yelped, "Hope whatever the doc does hurts, you mess-makin' sunuvabitch."

Lasher shuffled over to the sawbones's temporary examining table like a man on his last few paces to the gallows. He groaned and flopped into the waiting chair as though he'd just taken the final step on that fateful climb to ultimate doom. In spite of landing in an upright position, the injured murderer wobbled in the chair like a kid's top about to stop spinning.

Speaks poked around on the matted, bloody wound, slapped Lasher's hand away when the red-eyed brigand yelped and tried to object, then said, "Well, Quince, you mighta hit this poor, ignorant fool a bit harder than you seem to think. Gonna take ten or maybe fifteen stitches to sew this mess up. Way he's actin', you might've even concussed him a bit as well."

Bodine poked Bates on the arm. "Tole you 'at 'ere gash was worse'n you thought. Tole you, didn't I? Seen plenty of 'em in my time, and 'at 'un there's a doozie."

Lasher's bloodshot eyes rolled around in his head. "Damn right, you big, ugly, law-pushin' sunuvabitch. Mighta done went and *con-cussed* me. Turned my brains into somethin' akin to *huevos revueltos*. Hell, I might not ever be the same after the way you bounced that pistol barrel off'n my poor achin' skull. Ever' one a you law-bringin' cocksuckers always thinks you can just treat a man any which way you want and git away with it. Gonna suffer for whackin' me. Just you wait'n see, by God."

Bates hooked thumbs behind his webbed gun belt, grinned, then said, "Well, do the best you can with what you've got to work with there, Doc. No more'n he's got of 'em, sure as hell wouldn't want any of this idget's brains to leak out. Figure he's in possession of about half enough gumption to find the top of a black-powder pistol ball as it is."

Longarm added, "Fix 'im up good and proper, Doc. He's got a long trip back to Denver where he's gonna face the music for killin' hell out of a well-liked federal judge."

Lasher's eyes snapped open as though his befuddled mind had somehow instantaneously cleared up. A look of profound confusion swept over his unshaven, pockmarked face as he tried to push Doc Speaks's hand away. "Who the bleedin' fuck are you, mister?"

Longarm smiled. "Deputy U.S. Marshal Custis Long, Dolphus. I'm the man who has a warrant in his pocket for your arrest in the brutal and unnatural murder of Judge Elias Creed. The U.S. marshal in Denver can't wait to get his stubby-fingered little hands on your sorry hide, *pendejo*. Says he'll see you hang, sure's hell's hot and ice water's cold. Gonna personally watch you soil yourself 'fore God and a number of carefully chosen federal witnesses."

Of a sudden, Lasher assumed the behavior of a man who'd just awakened from a deep sleep. "Shit," he grunted. "Well, by God, that sure 'nuff cuts it. But I ain't so stupid or easy to get to the gallows as you seem to think, you star-wearin' bastard. Jus' might have a serious surprise for your long-legged, skinny-assed self 'fore this business all shakes out."

From across the room, Quincy Bates let out a derisive chuckle. "Only thing that'd surprise me or anyone else about you, Lasher, is if a bolt of lightning fell from a clear blue sky and turned you into a hymn-singing, traveling revivalist divinely bequeathed with the God-given power to save the eternal souls of every whiskey-swillin' repro-bate in the great Lone Star State."

Lasher spit on the floor. He glared at Bates like he wanted to rip the grinning marshal's ears off and stuff them up the mouthy marshal's ass.

Man obviously understands an insult when he hears it,

Longarm thought, *even if he is about half as smart as a wagonload of rocks.* To Longarm, Dolphus Lasher had the cold-eyed look of a man who would gladly kill everybody in the room, given half a chance.

Doc Speaks pushed Lasher's head to one side, then motioned for Longarm to step over and assist him. "Stop jawing around, mister, and let me get this mess fixed. Marshal Long, I'm gonna use these clamps to close this wound, then I'll stitch him up. Be of some help if you could hold these instruments out of my way whilst I suture this scalp lesion."

Even a casual observer would have easily noted that Lasher suffered like a centipede with a corn the size of a ten-dollar double eagle on the bottom of every foot. Man acted like he was being forced to endure the tortures of the damned. He whined, yelped, griped, and moaned during the entire ten-minute process.

When the ugly gash was finally cleansed and doused in carbolic and the last stitch tied, the arrogant brigand fingered the lumpy gash and mumbled, "Soon's my pap gets here, you sons a bitches gonna wish you'd never done this to me, by God. Have all your peckers in my pocket then."

Longarm, who'd started back for his chair, whirled around and snapped, "What'd you just say?"

Surprised that someone actually overheard what had just spilled out of his mouth, Lasher looked as though he'd been slapped in the face with a skunk's odiferous pelt. He shook his head and tried to act innocent. "Nothin'. Swear 'fore Jesus, didn't say nothin'."

Longarm stomped back over to the injured thug, bent down, and got right in his face. "Said somethin' about your pap comin' to town. That's what I heard, wasn't it? Ole Kermit's on his way to Devils River, ain't he? That's why you damn near rode a good horse to death gettin' your stupid self down here from Fort Stockton. And if Kermit's comin', that means the entire iniquitous family's probably gonna be gatherin' soon. Ain't that the way of it, Dolphus?"

Lasher gritted his teeth, turned away, and tried not to face the excited lawman. "Got nothin' more to say to none a you fuckin' lawdogs. Now get the hell outta my face, you sunuvabitch. Breath smells of cheap, rotgut whiskey."

Fisted hands on his hips, Longarm cast a head-shaking glance at Quincy Bates. "We've got more'n a little bit of trouble if this flea-brained idiot's father is on the way to town."

"How so, Custis?" Bates said. "I mean, Hell's bells, like everyone else in this part of Tejas, I've heard of Kermit Lasher, and this 'un here, and the entire family's penchant for murder and mayhem."

"Well, then, you know Kermit for what he's capable of doin'."

"No doubt a'tall. But that don't make me wanna swallow my tobacco by a long damn shot. Sure enough, I've heard as how the Lasher clan's gifted with committin' some real goose pimplers. Far as the local hoople heads are concerned, that could well be a real worrier. But Dolphus here and his old man don't scare me none. Men are men, and the Lasher boys can die just as easily as anyone else."

Longarm shook his head. "True enough, Quince. But you're just not considering the whole of the problem we've got if what this snake said is true. See, this boogery jackass and his pappy are just the beginning of the problem. Ole Dolphus here has a brother by the name of Obidiah. Most folks call the hulking brute Obie. And there's also a sister—believe her name's Ardella. I've heard tell she's tougher'n either one a Kermit's idget sons."

58

Dolphus Lasher let out a derisive giggle. "Oh, yeah, Ardella's a case-hardened gal alright. Been known to hunt wildcats with a fuckin' willow switch. But, truth is, she ain't nothin' but a fart in the wind compared to Obie. You jus' wait till Obie gets here. He'll kick the shit outta both a you law-pushin' sons a bitches."

Longarm let a tense, toothy grin play across his face. "Ah, so they are gatherin', and right here in Devils River. When they supposed to get here, Dolphus?"

"Fuck you, lawdog," Lasher snarled. "Ain't tellin' you another thang."

Custis Long ran a hand under his hat, scratched his head, then glanced back down at the smart-mouthed jackass just in time to see a look of sheer, determined panic play across Lasher's butt-ugly face. With no warning whatsoever, the freshly patched-up brigand bolted from his rough-built chair and tangle-footed it for the door.

The split-scalped thug barely managed a single clumsy step when Longarm kicked a leg out. Lasher tripped, flew through the air like an Apache war lance, and crashed headfirst into the jail's front door. With a resounding bone-crunching thump, he crumpled into a twitching heap, then rolled onto his back. Lasher's uglier-than-hammered-shit face sported a fresh, gruesome-looking wound across the bridge of his twisted, bloodied nose.

From across the room, Quincy Bates said, "Sweet Jesus, the man's a complete idiot."

Chapter 7

Longarm bent over, grabbed the semiconscious Lasher by the shirtfront, then dragged him back to the empty chair. With the doc's help, they got the wilted lout sitting up again.

Speaks shook his head, placed his satchel on the table again, and through a crooked grin said, "Damn. From the look of it, fellers, guess I might as well stick around a bit longer. Hell's bells, if this churnhead wakes up and does any more damage to himself, I could very well be here all afternoon."

Lasher groaned and blinked several times. A wild-eyed, confused look swept over his bruised and bloodied face. He shook a shaggy head like an old dog with a tick in its ear. Blood, snot, and spittle flew in every direction.

Longarm jumped as far away from the airborne discharge as he could. "Shit, Dolphus. Stop shakin' your head. You're makin' a helluva mess."

"Wha' the fuck happened," Lasher moaned, then gingerly ran trembling fingers up to his most recent mutilation. "God A'mighty, I'm a-bleedin' again. Whadda fuck'd you bastards do to me? Been a-whackin' on me again, ain't you? Ain't Christian, by God. I got rights, jus' like anyone else. Hell, yes, I got rights. Even if I am your prisoner, you ain't s'posed to be beatin' on me like I'm some kinda tied-up dog."

Speaks broke his bag open for the second time. He dragged out the necessary equipment—again. Poured fresh water in Quincy Bates's big washbowl—again. Then went to work on Lasher—again.

Ten more minutes of howling complaints, shouted curses, and pitiful whining finally ended when, needle and thread in hand, Speaks stepped aside. His hands and forearms up to his elbows were covered with blood. Lasher's black-eyed face looked like he'd just had a set of railroad tracks applied from the middle of his forehead down across his nose and onto one cheek.

Perched on the corner of Quincy Bates's banker's desk, Longarm said, "Christ, Dolphus, you've got a mug that looks like the reverse side of a recently stitched-together saddlebag."

Barely able to talk, Lasher grumped, "Ah thang you boys hit me whilst I wasn't lookin'. Tha's it. Done beat hell outta me from behin'."

"Don't really matter what you think at the moment, you stupid bag of horseshit. Need you to get back to the original question. When's your benighted family supposed to get to town?" Longarm snapped.

Quincy Bates called out, "Better yet, why're they comin' here in the first place? Why's the Lasher tribe gatherin' up in an out-of-the-way place like Devils River?"

Dolphus Lasher's bloodshot glance darted from one lawman to the other. He torqued his head to one side as though his neck hurt, then grunted. "Ain't shayin' nuthin' else to either of you bastards."

Grim faced, Quincy Bates drew his long-barreled, cavalry model Colt and strode to Lasher's side.

Lasher recoiled, hands raised in front of his face as

though sure he was about to be bludgeoned with the pistol. "Wha' you gonna do?" the wide-eyed gunny groaned.

"Answer Marshal Long's question, you belly-slinkin' snake. Otherwise I'm gonna put a wider, deeper, bloodier gash on the undamaged side of your melon-thick head to match that 'un Doc Speaks sewed up 'fore you tried to butt a hole in my door."

"You wouldn't," Lasher groaned.

"Oh, yeah? Maybe I'll step over on the other side and whack you so's you'll have a nice new slice across your nose to match the one you just put there yourself. Have a nice big X-shaped scar right in the middle of your ugly face then. Long as Doc's already here, might as well take advantage of the man's softhearted willingness to sew you back together."

"Hell you say," Lasher yelped. "Wouldn't go'n wallop me again for no reason. Not with two witnesses watchin'. 'Sides, you doan scare me none. Whackin' me once 'cause I tried to draw a pistol on somebody's one thing. This'd be a completely different animal altogether. Wouldn't bust me up for nothin'."

Colder than a well rope in Montana, Bates said, "Don't bet the ranch on it, Dolphus."

Lasher let out a derisive giggle. "Far as I'm concerned, you can take that big ole pistol and shove it up your more than stupid ass. Sideways. Then you can twist it."

Longarm slipped a fresh cheroot from his coat pocket and fired it up. Shook the match out, then from between clenched teeth, he said, "Don't know 'bout Doc Speaks, Dolphus, but a travelin' circus could roll through Marshal Bates's office right this very minute and I'm almost certain I wouldn't see a damned thing. Not even the lions, tigers, and elephants, exotic dancin' girls, the sword-swallowin' feller, or anything else. How 'bout you, Doc?"

Speaks appeared completely engrossed as he made something of a production out of, once again, stuffing medical implements back into his black, leather bag. "I'm not even here," the sawbones replied, and continued to poke around in the overflowing satchel. "Wouldn't be able to testify on any untoward event, no matter how brutal it might turn out. Man could have several fingers cut off and I wouldn't even notice."

Longarm turned to Hamp Bodine. "You see anything unusual, Hamp?"

Bodine grinned, then said, "Been havin' these here spells, you know. Blind spells. Cain't see a thing sometimes. Makes life right difficult. Bet I'd miss it if somethin' wayward was to happen to Mr. Lasher."

A grinning Quincy Bates did a fancy finger twirl with his pistol and slipped it back into a well-oiled holster. He reached around his back and slowly came out with a luminous, bone-handled bowie knife that looked every inch of a foot long from glistening tip to silver-capped grip. "Bet if we separated you from some of your more useless digits, you'd tell us anything we wanted to know, Dolphus. Maybe I'll take the little finger on each hand just to see how long you keep up with this arrogant-assed front you're puttin' up. Folks might start callin' you Eight-Fingered Lasher."

Bates stepped over to his desk and snatched up a sheet of writing paper. He slid the razor-sharp blade of the bowie through the blank page as though it were made of near-melted butter. The soft, sawing sound that emanated sent a chilling shiver through everyone in the room.

Lasher's bloodshot, blackened eyes got as big as saucers. "Sweet Jeezus."

Bates held the enormous knife up in front of his face and gazed at his own reflection. "She's razor-sharp, Dolphus.

Use this knife to shave with every morning. Year or so ago I nicked myself on the neck. Thought I'd bleed to death sure as shootin'."

Longarm flashed Bates a conspiratorial glance, then said, "She does look mighty keen to me, Quince. Bet it won't take more'n two or three slices to separate ole Dolphus from that itty-bitty trigger finger on his right hand."

Lasher stuffed a clenched fist between his legs and assumed the most pitiful and distressed look Longarm could ever recall seeing. "God A'mighty, you wouldn't dare do such a terrible thang. Cut off a man's trigger finger. Never heard of such, less it was done by them bloodthirsty Comanche."

"Oh, wouldn't we?" Bates sneered, then ran a thumb down the glistening blade's well-honed length. "Lord, it's sure 'nuff sharper'n the stinger on a Mexican hornet, alright. You've seen 'em, Dolphus. One a them big ole orange hornets that make you swell up and die right on the spot once they've stung you."

Lasher threw a pitiful, bug-eyed glance in Longarm's direction as though looking for support, comfort, maybe something in the way of protection. "You wanna take me back to Denver, Marshal? Cain't be showin' up with me all mutilated like I'd been attacked by bloodthirsty Indians of some kind. The U.S. marshal would have some mighty tough questions 'bout how such a thing could happen, I'd wager."

Longarm scratched his chin, then nodded. "Well, now, that's true, Dolphus, at least as far as it goes. But you know, I think Billy Vail would completely understand the necessity of separatin' you from a finger or three in the service of possibly savin' the lives of the innocent residents of Devils River. Don't you think so, Quince?"

"Oh, I'm absolutely sure of it, Custis," Bates said, then

darted to Lasher's side, grabbed the surprised brigand's right hand, and slammed it onto the chess table's top. Knights, bishops, and rooks flew off the table and onto the rough plank floor. Bates pulled the screeching gunny's little finger away from the rest and held the enormous, gleaming blade over the digit like a butcher about to dismember a chicken wing. "Give it up, Lasher, or I'll take your finger off right here and now."

"Oh, sweet Jesus, don't. Please," Lasher yelped.

Bates flashed an ugly snarl. "Get done with this here little 'un, go on to the next 'un. Once all your fingers are gone I'll start on your toes. Get 'round to your dick sooner or later."

"Shit. Shit. Oh shit. We know 'bout your bank," Lasher screeched. "Pap done foun' out 'bout your fuckin' bank, you sunuvabitch."

Quincy Bates's head snapped back as though he'd been slapped across the face with an open palm. He released the trembling hand and took a staggering step away from the table.

Lasher shook his fist at the stunned marshal. "That's right. That's fer damn sure right. Sure 'nuff, you big bastard. We know all 'bout Devils River's pissant-sized bank."

"How? How could you know anything 'bout our bank?"

Dolphus Lasher rubbed his wrist, twisted his hand about as though to make sure it was still attached. "How you think? Ain't no secret you can keep for the right price. Everthang's for sale."

Head cocked to one side, Longarm said, "What the hell's he talkin' about, Quince? What's there to know about Devils River's bank?"

Bates took an aggressive step back toward Lasher and waved the bowie under the grinning gunny's nose.

"You're lyin', Dolphus. If'n you know so damned much, tell Marshal Long what the hell you're talkin' about."

An evil, conspiratorial grin spread across Lasher's split, patched, bloodied, and bruised face. "First and third Monday a ever month, Great State Bank of Texas down in Del Rio ships a strongbox filled with solid gold coin up to Fort Lancaster, and then from there on to Fort Stockton. Not sure where it goes after that. Figure it somehow gets used to pay off all the bluebellies in this part a the state. Don't really matter. Anyway, special coach the box travels on usually stops overnight here in Devils River. Local bank keeps the money in its safe till the couriers can get back on the trail the next mornin'."

"He get it right, Quince?" Longarm asked.

Bates had the look of a man who'd put his bucket down a well and come up with a skunk. "Up till now what this low-life son of a bitch just said was the best-kept secret in all of Texas. Ain't a handful of people knew 'bout those shipments. Sure 'nuff begs the question of how'n the hell they found out about 'em."

Dolphus Lasher let out a mocking grunt. "Hell, that's the easiest part, Marshal. Ain't you never heard of the secret too big to keep? Well, that's what this is all about. Feller who used to drive them wagons up from Del Rio jus' happened to fall on hard times. Sold the information to my pap. And bein' as how today's Friday, Pap should be here jus' 'bout any time now. We's gonna take that gold shipment and live like kings down in Mexico for the rest of our natural lives."

"Think so?" Longarm said.

"Damned right. And they ain't nothin' either one a you badge-totin' bastards can do to stop it. Pap gets here he'll break me outta this cage, kill both a you bastards, and take whatever'n the blue-eyed hell he wants."

Longarm shot Quincy Bates a hot glance. "You got any deputies, Quince?"

Bates shook his head. "No. Just me'n Hamp. We're the only thing like law around here. You've seen the town. No need for any. Nothin' here of any real consequence. 'Cept the bank."

Longarm came to his feet, pulled his genuine Ingersoll railroader's pocket watch out for a look, then snapped the case closed and started for the door. He grasped the knob and pulled the heavy slab of wood open. He hesitated in the frame of light that spilled inside, turned back to Bates, and said, "Throw Dolphus's sorry ass back in his cage. Lock that outer door to the cell block. Get a Greener down from your weapons rack, load 'er up, and button this place up tight. Once Kermit arrives in town, it might get real woolly 'round here 'fore it gets better. Could be a rough couple a days and nights in Devils River 'fore this all shakes out. If the Lasher clan shows up, then death can't be far behind."

Longarm didn't waste any time hoofing it back to his hotel room. The snooty hotel clerk, who turned out be a gent named Horace Boykin, had made good on his word. As Longarm passed the outer desk, Boykin did his limp-wristed, dismissive wave again and said, "Your bath is ready, sir. Should be absolutely perfect by now."

Sure enough, a galvanized tub of froufrou-smelling water that had degraded to just the right temperature sat in the middle of his well-appointed room, awaiting his return.

And after a good scrub, a shave, a generous splash of bay rum, and a change into some almost clean clothing, Longarm dropped a pile of laundry off at the front desk, hit the dark, virtually deserted street again, and headed for Katy's Café. By that time the sun was nothing more than a glowing memory settling into the ocean on the far side of the world and the scorching temperature of that afternoon had subsided to the point where it was almost comfortable.

Flickering streetlamps here and there, assisted by the yellow-tinted glow cast from the windows of a few still-open businesses, offered some light. Overall, Devils River's central thoroughfare was in sore need of more in the way of illumination. Too many places to hide in the dark and ambush a man, Longarm thought as he trudged along.

Hard by the jailhouse's easternmost side, brightly lit and busy, Katy's Café appeared filled to overflowing with happy customers. Place bore a striking resemblance to a mud puddle in a rainstorm.

Powerful, nose-tickling aromas of fresh grilled beef, fried potatoes with onions, and buttermilk biscuits wafted from the open front door. *Guess I'll have something of a wait,* Longarm thought as he pulled the noisy establishment's screen door open and stepped inside.

A hefty, red-cheeked, smiling lady with a towel draped over her beefy shoulder and a steaming plate of food in each hand whizzed past, delivered her load, then quickly returned and stopped in front of Longarm as though sizing him up. She snatched the damp rag from her shoulder, wiped her chubby hands, and tilted her head to one side.

From behind twinkling eyes the color of slate, the sturdy lady said, "Well, now, Bell said you'd be comin' on by 'fore the night was over. Didn't bother to mention as how you're one fine-lookin' feller though." She held out a hand. "Name's Katy Tollifer, Mr. Long. Glad to have you."

Longarm removed his hat, flashed a toothy grin, shook the stout woman's still-damp hand, and nodded. "Most kind of you, ma'am. Miss Harvey suggested your fine establishment for a good meal." He glanced around the room and added, "Given the size of the crowd, and from what I can smell, I'd say she was correct."

Katy Tollifer tossed her head to indicate a spot in the back corner of the room near another open screen door. "Got a spot all set up and ready for you, good-lookin'. Right next to the exit where it's a bit cooler. Little bit of a breeze movin' from front to back kinda passes that way. Bell's a-waitin' for you."

The busy restaurant was so crowded Longarm hadn't noticed the beautiful blacksmith, and he probably never would have recognized the girl, given the surprising change in her appearance. Gone were the greasy leather apron and the filthy, sleeveless shirt. He figured she had probably abandoned the man's sailcloth pants as well, but couldn't tell for sure because the table covered her glorious figure from the waist down.

She'd scrubbed her face till it glowed, washed her hair, and applied just the least bit of lip rouge. Dressed in a wheat-colored, open-throated, sheer muslin blouse and a tight, short-waisted jacket that placed a dazzling expanse of her ample breasts on display, the girl looked as delicious as the cooking food in the kitchen smelled.

While Longarm couldn't see Bell's skirt, he assumed it probably matched the lighter, more comfortable wisp of a jacket. Near as he could tell, she'd chosen the simple, cool, and revealingly elegant outfit so the sight of her would hit a spot just below the buckle on his pistol belt and further stoke the growing conflagration in his balbriggans.

He shot the ebullient Katy Tollifer another friendly nod and, holding his hat over his freshly inflamed crotch, carefully made his way between the crowded tables of noisy patrons. The short walk turned into a tricky proposition, but he finally made it to the back of the room without revealing a boner the size of an ax handle.

Chapter 8

Bell Harvey smiled, graciously waved Longarm to an empty chair, and said, "Felt fairly certain you'd stop in, Marshal. Quite pleased you didn't disappoint me. Have a place all ready and waitin' for you, and our food is on its way to the table at this very moment."

The girl with the golden eyes had picked their meals from a list of only three choices that was scribbled on a chalkboard hanging over the window to the kitchen. His turned out to be a hearty, manly plate of steak and potatoes—hers a variety of fresh vegetables, guaranteed not to add unwanted pounds to an eye-catching shape.

With a three-tined fork poised over her plate, Bell Harvey flashed a million-dollar glance Longarm's direction, then said, "Hear tell our little out-of-the-way burg could well be in for some rough times. Way I heard it, ole Kermit Lasher's on his evil way to join up with his idiot son."

Longarm swallowed a tasty mouthful of grilled, perfectly charred, flame-kissed beefsteak, dabbed at his lips with a spotless napkin, then took a sip from the glass of freshly brewed tea beside his plate. As he set the amber-colored liquid aside, he sucked a morsel of food from between his teeth, then said, "'Pears as how word of potential events gets around mighty quick in Devils River. Had hoped Quincy wouldn't go off half-cocked and tell everyone in town. But what's done is done, I suppose."

Ruby-colored flecks embedded in Bell's bullion-colored eyes sparkled like tiny balls of fire when she said, "Doubt he told anyone else, Marshal Long. Only reason he told me is because I've known 'bout that Concord comin' up from the Valverde State Bank down in Del Rio for some time now."

"Really. And how did you ferret out that supposedly well-kept secret?"

"Well, while the bank and the U.S. Army did put considerable effort into trying to hide its actual purpose by disguising the whole deal as just another passenger run, the load that coach has to carry puts considerable stress on the thoroughbraces."

"Ah. Interesting, but I'm still in the dark."

"Expressmen on the coach've snapped several of 'em in the past, and I'm the one who replaced 'em. Most times you can't break much of anything on a Concord coach, much less a three-inch-thick thoroughbrace. The elm, oak, and ash running gear on those things is so well seasoned most of the wooden parts are actually more durable than iron. Just have to wear the individual parts out. Naturally untoward events, such as a broken thoroughbrace, on more than one occasion got my curiosity up."

She shoved a stingy forkful of snap beans into her full-lipped mouth, chewed them up, and swallowed, then added, "Didn't take much in the way of girly wiles and female persuasion to pry the secret out of ole Quincy. Bat my eyes, kinda lean up against him just the right way, and he'll tell me just about anything."

Longarm shook his head, then said, "Don't say much for us men, does it?"

"Very perceptive of you, Marshal Long. 'Course I kept what I discovered to myself. Guess Quincy appreciated that. He's been using me as a kind of secret sister confessor ever since. And, good God, the man does have an abundance of secrets to share. Leastways, that's what he seems to think."

Longarm took another sip of his tea, then arched an eyebrow. "That the extent of your relationship with Bates, Bell?"

"Why, Marshal Long, what on earth are you suggesting?"

"Oh, nothing. Nothing at all, I assure you."

"Sounds to me like you might be jealous."

"No, 'course not, darlin'. Don't know you well enough to be jealous. Just wanted to make sure I'm not steppin' on anyone's toes by showing up here tonight and havin' supper with you. Never have cared for the possibility of being shot by a jealous husband or lover."

It surprised Longarm just a mite when Bell leaned closer and almost whispered, "Never mind any of the other men in Devils River." She shot him a wicked, leering glance. "Hope you've got something appropriately carnal in mind for after supper."

Bell Harvey's blatant invitation was delivered in the sultriest of tones and with the kind of look that welded Longarm to his chair. For about a second he didn't move, but after the passage of that short interval their meal proceeded to an end in a right speedy fashion. As Longarm took his last bite, he dropped his napkin onto an empty plate and said, "Good thing nobody got in the way of my knife and fork after what you said a while ago, gal. I'd a carved 'em up like trussed chickens."

In less than half an hour, by Longarm's genuine, two-dollar, railroader's pocket watch, the anxious couple had polished off their meal, then hurriedly excused themselves from Katy's Café. The handsome pair walked arm in arm in the dim, yellow-tinted light cast from the windows of the smattering of still-active Devils River businesses. They crossed the deserted main thoroughfare, stepped onto the boardwalk in front of the once showy music hall, then ambled in the general direction of Davis House.

"You sure 'bout this, Bell?" Longarm said.

She leaned her tall, lanky bulk against him. Took no more than half a dozen steps for Longarm to become acutely aware of the strength and suppleness of the beautifully muscled body pressed to his. He became conscious of a breast every bit as big around as a three-pound cannonball. After some careful consideration on the subject, he could even detect an erect nipple the size of a man's thumb very deliberately being rubbed back and forth across the flexed muscle of his upper arm.

The scent of magnolia blossoms, along with a swirl of ripe, juicy, excited female musk, rose from Bell Harvey's body. The tart, animalistic bouquet oozed up from between tawny thighs and easily passed through the sheer, wheat-colored muslin skirt clinging to her long, shapely legs. The heavy, sweet aroma of her sex tickled the edges of Longarm's nose, inflamed his desire, then shot down his belly to the rapidly stiffening crowbar of love once again straining at the crotch of his skintight tweed pants.

At a particularly dark spot on the boardwalk, in the opening of an alleyway between the Devils River Music Hall and the Texas State Land Office, Bell Harvey used her nearly six-foot frame to muscle Longarm up against the wall. Then she brought her hips up and ground her steaming crotch against his now rock-hard prong. On top

76

of a flurry of rapid-fire hunching, she threw an arm around his neck, pulled his face to hers, and slapped a sloppy, openmouthed, tongue-darting lip-lock on him. Felt as though she might suck the tongue right out of his head before she broke the kiss.

When she finally let him up for air, Longarm gasped, then said, "Kinda forward of you there, Bell."

She ran an inquisitive hand down the front of his straining trousers, squeezed his enormous doinker, then socked her steamy notch up against him again. "Can't help it. I've always liked the way it feels when a man gets excited, gets hard, gets to wantin' me. Makes me wet, and good God, I love bein' wet."

"Hey, whatever stokes your engine just suits me right down to the ground."

"Figured it would," she said, then filled his mouth with her snaky tongue again.

She broke the kiss, then whispered, "But don't be misled, Custis. This isn't my usual conduct with most men. Just that there's not much to choose from around these parts, and, sweet mother of pearl, it's been quite a dry spell since my last ride."

Longarm gently clasped Bell's arm just above the elbow and urged the obviously horny gal back onto the boardwalk. She let out a huffing snort of pleasure at his mildly rough treatment, wrapped one arm around his waist, then made a mighty effort at jamming her free hand inside his pants. She nibbled at his neck. Bit and licked his ear inside and out, then whispered, "Step into the recess created by the entrance to Bloom's Variety Store and I'll suck you dry."

While her blatantly carnal proposal was a more than tempting offer, Longarm had other ideas. He hustled her down the alley between an abandoned dress shop and the hotel. They entered the Davis House through a back entrance and managed to make it to his room without being detected.

As he keyed the lock, the randy woman started pawing at the crotch of his pants again, at the same time whispering, "How gallant of you to consider my reputation with the locals, Marshal Long. Guess it wouldn't do for one of the ladies from the local Baptist church to spot me in an alley sucking the cock of a stranger."

Then Bell Harvey attached herself to Longarm like a she-wolf in heat. Her lecherous efforts caused him to stumble as they crossed the threshold. Barely a step inside the room, she turned him loose, snatched at the waist of her flimsy skirt, and quickly shucked the entire thing in one sweeping, near magical wave of the arm. The diaphanous article of clothing floated to the floor like a drifting leaf on an October breeze and was immediately followed by her matching blouse and jacket.

To Longarm's utter surprise she wore not a single stitch beneath either delicate, ultrafeminine garment. In a pool of pale gray that fell from the fingernail sliver of moonlight that dropped through the room's windows, the hungry-eyed, lust-addled girl stood with legs spread wide. One hand was going like crazy in the thick, triangular patch of coal-black hair between her quivering thighs, while the other worked on the bullet-hard nipple of one enormous, upturned breast.

Completely aroused by such brazen behavior, Longarm unbuckled his cartridge belt as quickly as he could manage the move and dropped the entire rig onto the floor. His hat, jacket, tie, and shirt went next. As he shed his pants and balbriggans, his gigantic wand of love flipped up and slapped against his belly with a resounding smack. Even in the poorly lit room, he saw Bell Harvey's eyes widen, and noticed that the hand between her legs appeared to speed up in her brazen efforts to inflame him even further.

"Oh, sweet Jesus," the panting girl hissed, "come and get it, big boy."

Barely two steps were necessary to bring his mouth to the stiffened, erect nipple the lecherous female had so conveniently left exposed. She moaned into Longarm's exposed ear while his tongue danced around the hardened point of sensitive flesh, then she set to sucking on the other nipple herself.

Longarm pushed the hand between her legs aside and substituted his own. She gasped when his fingers found the throbbing, secret button to the very core of her being. Her gasping sighs became even more pronounced when she closed trembling fingers around a dingus that seemed to have the size and texture of a hickory hatchet handle.

Of a sudden, Bell yelped, "Oh, God," then dropped to her knees and engulfed the massive head of Longarm's throbbing prong with her moist lips. She swallowed down as much of the steely love muscle as she was able, but had to give up about halfway along the shaft.

After several minutes of nerve-jangling licks, sucks, and kisses, Bell's rosy lips came away with a loud, wet smack. Longarm reached down, grasped the leering girl under her arms, and lifted her up as high as he could. Her lanky, muscular legs encircled his waist as he slowly lowered her juice-dripping snatch onto the tip of his turgid tool.

When Longarm's swollen rod of joy finally hit the bottom of Bell's steaming cooch, she yelped, threw her arms around his neck, gasped, then cut loose with a noisy, squirting, orgasmic gush. Then, to his complete surprise, her arms dropped to her sides. Bell's gold-colored eyes rolled back and her head lolled to one side as though she'd lost total contact with reality.

For several seconds the enthusiastic woman appeared to have passed out completely. Then, just as suddenly, she snapped back into the situation like a lust-addled female tiger. She uncoiled her legs from around Longarm's waist and pulled away long enough to push him back onto the bed. With total abandon, she leapt on top of the prostrate lawdog, grabbed his thick root, guided it into her dripping snatch, and proceeded to ride his wondrous prong like a South Texas brush popper astride a wildly bucking bronco.

Near an hour into the sweaty, ass-busting ride, she suddenly hopped off his inflamed tool, hunched all the way up to Longarm's waiting tongue, squatted over his face, and shuddered as though in the throes of a killer malaria attack. Once he'd found the perfect spot and licked her until she'd fallen into near insensibility, the sex-besotted girl crammed both hands into her sweltering crotch and helped him bring on what appeared to rate as a second earth-shattering climax.

Spent and appearing near exhaustion, Bell rolled away from Longarm's busy tongue, both hands still buried in her frothy glory hole. He propped himself up on one elbow and watched as she energetically massaged herself to a third and final intense, shuddering orgasm. Within minutes the sated girl drew into a tight ball and was snoring like a two-man, crosscut saw ripping its way through knots in a hundred-year-old oak tree.

Feeling more than a little used, in spite of the beautiful Bell's energetic efforts, and perhaps just a bit short of satisfied, Longarm crawled out of the sweat-saturated bed, covered the sleeping girl with a sheet, then threw a quilt over his own shoulders. He silently padded across the floor, grabbed a nickel cheroot from his coat pocket, then rummaged around and dragged a half-empty bottle of Maryland rye out of his possibles bag.

While trying not to disturb his sleeping guest, he wrapped himself in the blanket, then tiptoed over to the set of French doors that led to the balcony. Once outside, he flopped into one of the cushioned chairs and placed his bottle on the rugged table.

He shook the match used to light the square-cut cheroot to death, then flicked it into the deserted street below. The tart smoke from the fresh cigar tasted pretty good when mixed with Bell Harvey's sticky love juice.

Devils River was graveyard quiet. Longarm couldn't see a living soul out on the street. Even the dogs appeared to have skulked away. The sun's fiery departure from a cloudless sky had resulted in a rapid but invigorating cooling that felt mighty good after the scorching day. After two or three pulls on the bottle, he drifted off into a sound, dreamless sleep.

Sometime in the predawn Longarm snapped awake. Bell still snored away in the room. For reasons that could only be attributed to a deeply ingrained sense of deadly intuition, he glanced toward the west end of the main thoroughfare. In the dim light provided by a rapidly waning moon, the figures of five riders, draped in the ghostly garb of long, white linen dusters, slowly made their silent, eerie way up the empty street. Covered with a fine layer of dust, their spectral mounts appeared to glide along the empty street as though not of this world.

The unexpected, cold, prickling sensation of gooseflesh running up his back caused Longarm to sit bolt upright in his chair and lean forward in a pose of finely focused concentration. He rubbed sleep-caked eyes to make sure he wasn't still napping and simply fighting off a bad dream.

From the privacy of his unnoticed vantage point, Longarm watched, spellbound, as the sinister gang moseyed past Bell Harvey's stable, an abandoned liquor store, the derelict shell of a deserted firehouse, Steed's Dry Goods Emporium, and the Rusty Pump saloon. They finally reined their phantom plugs up in front of the dilapidated Cattleman's hotel. Devils River's main street was so quiet a man of Longarm's sensibilities could easily smell death coming.

From his unseen perch, just two doors down and across the street from the Cattleman's, Longarm had an unrestricted view of the ominous bunch. Trying his best not to move or draw any unwanted attention to himself, he watched as the riders boldly stepped down from their haggard, otherworldly animals, tied them to a convenient hitch rail, retrieved rifles and saddlebags, then clomped onto the boardwalk and into the meager light that oozed from the hotel's large front window.

No doubt about it in Longarm's mind. The leader of the group was none other than Kermit Lasher. The man could not possibly have been mistaken for anyone else. Tallest of the group, pale, white-bearded, and gaunt, Lasher stood away from the light and testily motioned for the others to move inside the hotel.

Wide as a doubled-up barn door and almost as tall as the old man, an imposing figure Longarm took to be Obidiah pushed his way inside first. Obie Lasher was a giant of a man and a force to be reckoned with.

Sister Ardella, dressed in the rough riding garb of a man, snatched off her tall-crowned Stetson, shook loose a flowing mane of tawny hair, and followed Dolphus's massive brother inside.

The fourth and fifth members of the gang stopped before entering the hotel, then cast menacing glances up and down the street. Longarm couldn't quite make out the pair's faces because their wide-brimmed, palm-leaf sombreros obstructed much of his view. As the unrecognized gunnies moved off the boardwalk, Kermit Lasher pulled his duster back to reveal the glint of silver-mounted pistols.

Longarm grunted and carefully slipped the bottle of rye from the tabletop as Kermit Lasher glared around at nothing in particular, then disappeared from view like a wisp of evil fog carried away on invigorating breezes.

Longarm leaned back in his chair and took another healthy drag on the bottle. For more than an hour he sat, wrapped in the quilt, scratching his chin and trying to reason out which way the wind might blow once the elder Lasher realized his plans for the Del Rio gold shipment might have hit a serious snag. He finally decided there was just no way to know the future other than to recognize that with a crew like ole Kermit's bunch in town, wicked doin's in Devils River were pretty much a foregone conclusion. He took another pull on the bottle, set it on the floor, and scrunched down in the chair. No need worryin' till mornin', he thought, then drifted into a restful and much-needed few hours of peaceful sleep.

Chapter 9

A sliver of morning sunlight sliced through the curtain of
escaping night and pried Longarm's reluctant eyes open.
Still wrapped in the blanket and seated in the chair on the
veranda, his capped bottle of rye rolled off his lap and
thumped to a spot near his foot as he stood. The heady
aromas of frying bacon, eggs, and fresh-baked biscuits
wafted up from Katy's Café on a barely perceptible
breeze. Through the dusty morning's haze, the groggy
lawdog noted that the Lasher gang's forlorn bangtails still
stood at the hitch rail in front of the Cattleman's.

Feeling like death warmed over, Longarm stretched
his kinked spine. Individual vertebrae snapped into place
like links in a logging chain. He yawned, then snatched
the half-empty bottle up and hobbled back into his room.
Bell Harvey had somehow managed to slip away unnoticed. The bedsheets felt cold to the touch, but the musky
aroma of her dripping sex still hung in the air and clung
to his aching body like a second skin. Girl had damned
near ridden him into the ground, dropped off to sleep like
an overworked lumberjack, and then abandoned the scene
like a skulking thief.

Appeared to Longarm that concerns over the propriety of their carnal tussle weighed heavily enough on the beautiful gal to send her into the street before the sun came up in an effort to keep local gossip to a minimum. He stared at the empty bed and shook his head. Just nothing like the nattering blather of backyard gossips to ruin a woman's reputation—even if there might only be a handful of them left in town.

After a cold-water rinse, a lightning-fast shave, and half-assed effort to straighten up his disheveled room, a semirefreshed Custis Long, smelling of bay rum and tobacco, stepped onto the boardwalk in front of Davis House. He fired a nickel cheroot, flicked the still-burning match into the street, then leaned against a porch pillar just in time to catch sight of one of the two men in the Lasher party that he hadn't quite been able to recognize the night before. The hulking brute staggered from the Cattleman's front entrance, gathered up the reins of all the animals at the hitch rail, and started leading them toward Bell Harvey's stable.

"Christ," Longarm groaned through gritted teeth, then turned on his heel and legged it for Katy's Café. He took his time eating that morning and had hoped Bell Harvey would eventually come by, but she didn't show. After a meal of six scrambled eggs, half a dozen biscuits and gravy, eight strips of bacon, a pint of jalapeño jelly, a cup of coffee, and three glasses of buttermilk, the achy-muscled lawdog felt much better than he looked as he pushed open the door of Marshal Quincy Bates's office and stepped inside.

Slumped in his squeaking banker's chair, hair a mass of sleep-generated tangles, Devils River's bleary-eyed lawman nursed a cup of steaming stump juice and glanced up as though surprised when Longarm burst in. He grinned and sounded pleased when he said, "Damned if you don't look like you've been run down, run over, and wrung out, Custis. Musta had a rough night."

Longarm grimaced, then strode directly for the coffeepot. "You should talk," he said, then poured himself a tin cup of the potent belly wash, blew on the hot liquid for several seconds, then downed a healthy swig before saying, "Trust me when I tell you that *I'm* not quite as bad off as you might think. More important, thought you might like to know that I spent most of last night sittin' on the balcony of my room and watchin' the street. Spotted the Lasher bunch when they rode in 'bout two this mornin'. Whole damned crew put up at the Cattleman's. Watched 'em file in and they didn't come out."

"You saw 'em?" Bates sat up straight but didn't exactly sound as though stricken with terror. Definitive news of the Lasher gang's arrival, and the fact that the unpredictable bunch was staying in a hotel barely six doors down the main thoroughfare from his office, appeared not to have hit the man all that hard.

"Well, have to admit, I'd had a snort or two 'fore I spotted 'em. Pretty sure it was Kermit, Obie, Ardella, and a couple a other fellers I didn't recognize at the time. You can piss in my hat, and I'll hold it for you while you fill it up if it ain't them."

"Whataya mean, didn't recognize some of 'em at the time?"

"Too dark in the street last night, Quince. Like I said, saw 'em ride in, but I just didn't know who two of 'em were. Mighta had a few more swigs on the jug than I thought. Anyhow, this mornin', when I stepped out on the boardwalk in front of Davis House, I got a better look at one of 'em, and I'm pretty sure it was Honas Clinch."

Hamp Bodine groaned like a man who'd just been hit with a double-bit ax. "Honas Clinch? You're sure? Sweet merciful Jesus. Honas Clinch."

Quincy Bates shot Longarm an inquisitive, puzzled glance. "Hell, Custis, Honas Clinch's uglier'n a gunny sack full a assholes. Ain't much of a way to mistake him for someone else. Unless . . ."

Longarm nodded. "Unless the man I saw was Honas's equally ugly brother, Boggs—the one most folks who have eyes refer to as Booger. The one known all over Texas as the kind who enjoys beatin' a man to death with his bare hands. That one."

Bates rolled his eyes and let his head loll from side to side. "Fuckin' figures. Just fuckin' figures. Not bad enough ole Kermit and his other two knuckleheaded offspring show up. Oh, no. He brings a pair of the most infamous brigands and troublemakers in all of Tejas along with him."

Longarm sucked another sip of the scalding liquid down and made a face as though he'd just stuck his tongue in a cup of scalding horse piss.

From the doorway of the cell block, Hamp Bodine growled, "Ain't no point a makin' faces at my coffee, Marshal Long. Best you're gonna git around these here parts. Let Quince anywhere near a coffeepot and you get somethin' akin to mud-colored wallpaper paste."

"Didn't hear me complainin', did you, Hamp?"

"No. No, I didn't, Marshal Long. Jest wanted to let you know it wouldn't do any good in case you decided to start."

Bates nursed his own cup, then squirmed in his squeaking chair and shook his head. "Tell the God's truth, Long, I had actually fooled myself into hopin' that ole Dolphus was just spinnin' out a blowhard's windy whizzer to try and impress us. Never for one second believed the old man and the others would actually put in an appearance. Shit a'mighty, that gang a cutthroats takes it in mind to do anything wayward and we just might be in for a world of hurt here."

From back in the cell block Dolphus Lasher yelled,

"Guess you badge-wearin' bastards'll perk up and listen from now on when I tell you somethin', won't you? Pap finds out you've got me locked up in this cow country calaboose he'll squash you law-bringin' sons a bitches like a pair a shit-rollin' dung beetles. Gonna be a sight to see. Cain't wait fer the dance to start, by God."

Over his shoulder, Bates yelled back, "Best shut the hell up, Dolphus. Wouldn't want me to come back there and stomp a ditch in your sorry ass, then turn around and stomp it dry."

Longarm flopped into the tack-decorated leather guest chair in front of Bates's desk. "Figure it wouldn't do any good to hit the trail runnin' for Denver with that stupid jackass in tow. Not right now anyway. Probably wouldn't get twenty miles 'fore the old man caught up with us, killed the hell outta me, and then set Dolphus loose."

"Well, they ain't gettin' in here, that's for damn sure," Bodine offered. "Walls a this lockup are built outta railroad cross ties held in place with steel retainin' rods thick as a San Francisco stevedore's wrists. It'd take ten sticks a dynamite to blow a hole in one a these walls. If'n we don't wanna let 'em inside, they ain't gettin' in, by God."

"True enough, but that means at least one of us is gonna have to stay inside all the time," Longarm said, then took another nibbling sip of Bodine's potent belly wash. "Anyone else you can enlist to help out, Quince? Another deputy, or even two, maybe?"

Bates stared into his cup as though lost in thought. "Might know at least one feller who'd help us out, but it'd be a stretch to find any assistance once everyone ferrets out the fact that the Lasher bunch is actually in town. Soon as news like that makes the rounds, just knowin' them sons a bitches are here is gonna scare the hell outta most folks."

"What about the coach from Del Rio, Quince?"

"Done took care a that problem."

"Really? How?"

"Sent a telegram to the bank officials down there late yesterday afternoon. Might seem like a slipshod operation, but we do have contingency plans for emergency situations. Valverde Bank's gonna reroute the shipment over through Rock Springs, then up to the railroad depot in Sonora and from there on over to Fort Lancaster. Might take a day or two longer, but that pile a money won't be comin' through Devils River, that's fer damned sure."

Longarm pushed back in his chair. "So, looks like Dolphus is our only real problem right now."

Bates let a mocking smile etch its way across his open, handsome face. "Helluva problem, Custis. Only question is, how long's it gonna be 'fore the fur starts to fly?"

Quincy Bates's ominous query still hung in the air when the jailhouse door popped open. A haggard-looking, one-armed man wearing a faded blue service jacket and a Grand Army of the Republic campaign cap sporting an artillery insignia limped across the threshold. He gingerly closed the door, then snatched off his battered cap. His near-hairless head bobbled as though in greeting, but he didn't say anything.

After a moment of strange, awkward silence, Hamp Bodine said, "What's up, Homer? Got somethin' on your mind?"

The elderly, toothless soldier nervously tapped his leg with the cap as he said, "Ain't usually given to meddlin' in other people's business."

Bodine threw a dismissive wave at the former artilleryman, then said, "We know that, Homer, but if you've got somethin' to say, just spit it on out."

"Well, I just thought maybe you fellers might wanna know as how they's a couple a mean-lookin' sorts that I ain't never seen afore down at the Rusty Pump a-beatin' the bejabbers outta that pianner-playin' feller, Elton Jackson."

Quincy Bates placed his empty cup on the desk, then stood. "Now why'n the blue-eyed hell would anybody wanna beat on Elton Jackson? Man's gotta be the most inoffensive human being and piano player I've ever been around. Plays some of the best music you can hear in a saloon, too. Heard tell the man has some kinda classical music background. Know for damned sure you can't hear his kinda ivory ticklin' in any other saloon in town. Probably in the whole damned state."

Longarm closed his eyes, pinched the bridge of his nose, and said, "Bet everything I'll make for the next year it's one or both of the Clinch brothers. Mighty early in the day for such shenanigans, but they're probably just sendin' a message to the local lawman that they're in town and not to be trifled with. Sure as hell didn't take 'em long. Thought maybe we'd get through at least one peaceful day 'fore the dance started. Guess I was wrong."

The color boiled up from under Quincy Bates's shirt collar—turned his neck and ears a bright red. "Well, by God, whoever them boys are, they're in my town today, and I won't put up with such behavior. Anything else, Homer?"

"Nope, that's it, Marshal."

Bates flipped the old soldier a coin, then said, "Why don't you go on down to Zang's and have yourself a drink. We'll take care of them boys in the Pump."

Homer stuffed his cap on, touched the brim, nodded, and vanished like a puff of cannon smoke.

Longarm stared into his cup. "Best be ready to go to the mat with men like the Clinch brothers, Quince. Only thing their kind understands is brute force, applied without anything resembling mercy."

"How would you handle this situation, Custis?"

"You let 'em get the upper hand and they'll drive you to drink, or kill you 'fore it's all over and done. I'd get on their heads like ugly on an armadillo, and I'd do the deed

91

so fast their wormy brains would still be swimmin' tomorrow mornin'."

Bates hopped to his feet, turned to the gun rack behind his desk, and pulled down two short-barreled shotguns. One he delivered into the anxious hands of Hamp Bodine and the other to Longarm. "They're loaded with buckshot," he said, then pulled a third weapon out for himself. "Bolt the front door soon's we're outside, Hamp. Then I want you to get inside the cell block. Close the entry gate and throw the bar. Don't let anyone but me or Marshal Long inside the office or back there. Understand?"

Bodine flashed a broad, snaggle-toothed grin, then said, "Damn right. Won't be nobody a-comin' into my cell block but you or Marshal Long, Quince. Swear 'fore Jesus, I'll put lead in anyone who makes it past the front door, or even tries."

Bates snatched a wide-brimmed, Mexican palm-leaf hat off a peg on the wall and stuffed it on his head. He strode around the desk, tapped Custis Long on the shoulder, then said, "Why don't we just stroll on down to the Rusty Pump and have a talk with the Clinch brothers. Read 'em the riot act accordin' to the town marshal of Devils River, Texas. Think between the two of us we can make God-fearin' believers out of 'em, right quick. 'Sides, would do my personal sense of self-worth a world a good to kick the hell outta anyone who'd beat on a man as harmless as Elton Jackson."

Longarm got to his feet, breeched the big popper, checked the massive brass-sleeved shells, then snapped it shut. "Well, Quince, let's go shake the Clinch brothers' tree and see what falls out."

Bates flashed a toothy smile. "Damned right. Let's do 'er."

Chapter 10

Hamp Bodine pushed the jailhouse door closed and threw the bolt behind the two lawmen as they stepped onto the boardwalk. "You boys call out 'fore you try to come back inside. Wouldn't want to put a hatful a lead in the wrong folks," he yelled through the heavy door.

Custis Long grinned at the old coot's hard-edged bluster and stepped into the street beside Quincy Bates just as Bell Harvey rushed up like a Mexican hornet with its stinger out. Once again dressed in her leather apron, man's pants, and sleeveless shirt, she had the look of a woman who could bite chunks off an anvil and spit horseshoe nails. Angry or passionate, fully dressed or buck-assed naked, the woman's unvarnished beauty had the power to take a man's breath away.

Since his mama didn't raise a melon-headed, water-brained, slobbering idiot, Longarm recognized a potential confrontation when he saw it coming. The fast-thinking lawdog took several steps away from Quincy Bates as the red-faced girl got right in the surprised town marshal's face and shook her finger at him.

"A butt-ugly piece of walking scuz, sportin' a mug like a map for the Southern Pacific Railroad, strolled into my place leadin' five horses soon's I cracked the door open this mornin'. In a matter of minutes that hulkin' piece of hammered cow shit proved he wouldn't know good manners if they slapped him in the face."

"Got a droopy eye? And I mean a real bad droopy eye. Almost like one side a his face got melted and sagged down toward his big dumb ass?" Longarm asked.

Devils River's stunningly beautiful stable owner and blacksmith swung her teeth-grinding glare Longarm's direction. "Well, he did look just about like his whole head had been set afire, then put out with a Comanche war ax. You know the filthy-mouthed, wicked stack of human waste, Custis?"

Longarm toed at the dusty street. "Not on what I'd call an actual shake-and-howdy basis, Bell. But if my reasonably accurate description fit, and from your reaction appears as how it did, sounds like Honas Clinch to me."

"Honas Clinch? What'n the hell's a Honas Clinch?" Bell snorted.

"A real bad sort, darlin'. Kinda feller you don't wanna cross. Not even on his best day."

Quincy Bates reached out and patted the angry woman on the shoulder, and promptly got his hand slapped away.

"Don't be pattin' on me, Quincy," she snapped.

"Look, Bell," he said, "me'n Longarm are on our way over to the Rusty Pump right now. Seems both the Clinch brothers are in there whippin' up on little Elton Jackson."

Bell threw her head back, raised sooty arms to heaven in supplication, then glared at Bates and said, "Why'n the wide, wide world would anyone wanna beat on Elton Jackson? Wait, you mean there's two of 'em ugly sons of Satan?"

Longarm rested the heavy shotgun on his shoulder. "Yeah. Second one's named Boggs, but most folks call him Booger, if they bother to talk to him at all. Think maybe Kermit Lasher sent the two of 'em out to see just how much local law enforcement would put up with 'fore anyone reacted to their special kind of 'treatment.'"

Bell's gaze narrowed on Longarm. "Lasher's actually in town?"

Quincy Bates pushed Bell aside and motioned for Longarm to follow. "Yep, 'pears the whole damned clan's taken up residence over at the Cattleman's," he said, "and we're on the way over to the Pump to let Lasher's henchmen know that Devils River ain't the place to be messin' with the law. Think they're gonna be jerked up kinda short when I walk into the Pump backed up by a deputy U.S. marshal."

As the two lawmen tipped their hats and ambled away, Bell Harvey called out, "Be careful, both of you. Yellow-toothed animal who showed up in the stable this mornin' isn't the kind of creature to take kindly to any form of instruction on manners."

Shotguns at the ready, Longarm and Bates strode past the imposing Valverde State Bank, two abandoned buildings sporting roughly boarded-up windows, a still-active dry goods store, the telegraph office, and the Cattleman's hotel. Here and there a lone, drooping hay burner stood at a hitch rail, but the street appeared virtually bereft of people.

The Rusty Pump saloon lay hard by the Cattleman's hotel on its westernmost side, and looked like a carefully planned exact opposite of the more elegant Matador directly across the rutted, dusty street. The cow country cantina's rough-cut, board-and-batten facade's only nod toward anything like elegance was a pair of brightly painted, bloodred batwings that matched the equally gory-looking sign splashed across the single-pane glass-front window on the right side of the swinging doors. The rinky-tink sound of a frantically played piano flowed from the bar's darkened interior atop a wave of raucous laughter and ham-fisted table pounding.

Longarm stepped up on the boardwalk beside Marshal Quincy Bates. As the prickly pair of law bringers drew up outside the saloon's entrance, Longarm glanced over Bates's shoulder toward the front door of the Cattleman's, just to make sure no other members of the Lasher bunch might be lurking nearby.

His gaze welded to the darkened interior of the dram shop above the saloon doors, Bates leaned toward Longarm and whispered, "I'll go in first, Custis. Bar's on the right. Row of four or five tables on the left. Piano's in the back of the room. Shoved up in the corner on the left. Probably best if you take up a position at this end of the bar. That way you can see anyone who might come in behind us and you can cover me at the same time. I'll head left, get as close as I can, and, hopefully, brace 'em 'fore they have any real chance to react. You ready?"

Longarm nodded, grinned, and said, "Let 'er buck, Quince. You're covered."

Bates pushed his way through the swinging doors first. Shotgun cocked and ready for action, Longarm followed on the determined marshal's heels. As Bates strode to the middle of the room, Longarm moved directly to his assigned spot at the end of a coarse bar that didn't amount to much more than a set of rough-cut, two-by-twelve pine planks laid across the tops of several empty whiskey barrels.

Cigar and cigarette burns, carved initials, and myriad scars of undeterminable origin decorated the bar's crude top. A crop of green-tarnished, hard-used brass spittoons sprouted from the floor beneath the bar and popped out along the wall behind each of the five tables like gigantic, globular, swamp-dwelling mushrooms.

Every available bit of the Rusty Pump's wall space

sported some form of brush-popper apparel or equipment. A museum-worthy collection of hats, boots, spurs, quirts, stovepipe chaps, saddles, and the occasional stuffed animal made it difficult for the casual observer to tell the color of the wall behind. Near as Longarm could tell, the saloon's preferred clientele was obviously of the hardworking, ranch-hand variety, which went a long way to explain why the joint was open so early in the day.

Longarm's keen glance revealed that only four people inhabited the narrow room. The Rusty Pump's wild-eyed drink slinger had pressed himself up against the sparsely supplied back bar. On the wall behind the nervous beer wrangler hung a tattered, faded print of a busty, crimson-lipped blonde reclining nude and wrapped in something diaphanous, billowing, and purple. The clearly agitated bar dog had the look of someone who might bolt from the scene if given any reasonable opportunity.

Honas Clinch had seated his massive bulk at the table next to the piano and was leaning back in a rickety chair in order to place himself within easy, face-slapping reach of the bloody-eared Elton Jackson. Appeared to Longarm that Clinch had rapped the miniature instrumentalist across the chops more than once.

Boggs, Clinch's larger, uglier brother, leaned against the bar on one elbow, whiskey bottle in hand. The bear-like man was locked in the midst of a gut-slapping guffaw at the obvious discomfort of the diminutive, keyboard-pounding musician. None of the bar's preoccupied residents seemed to have heard or detected the lawmen's entry over the riotous thumping of the tinny-sounding upright piano.

The whole room jumped as though slapped when Quincy Bates growled at the top of his lungs, "What the hell you boys up to?"

The rowdy piano music abruptly stopped. Of a sudden,

the Rusty Pump saloon turned quieter than the bottom of a fresh-dug grave at midnight.

Honas Clinch brought his straight-backed, cane-bottomed chair down to the floor with a resounding thump. The much-abused piano player slammed the instrument shut, heeled it for a door in the back wall, and disappeared into the alley between the Rusty Pump and the Cattleman's.

The panicked bartender edged his way along the back bar, then hoofed it Longarm's direction and vanished through the batwings. The sound of the bar dog's fading footsteps could be heard as he pounded down the boardwalk toward the marshal's office.

Missing its cork, the open liquor bottle slipped from Boggs Clinch's fingers, landed upright on the filthy floor beneath his feet, and squirted a stream of whiskey waist high. Boggs watched his brother struggle to get himself standing. Both men turned on Devils River's marshal as their skillet-sized hands fumbled with filthy dusters to expose an array of crossed, bullet-laden pistol belts and well-oiled revolvers.

"Who the fuck are you?" a swaying Honas Clinch barked.

"Yeah," Boggs chimed in through rotted teeth, "who the fuck are you, mister?"

"Name's Quincy Bates, boys. Marshal Quincy Bates. Gent standin' behind me to my right is Deputy U.S. Marshal Custis Long."

The deep-set, animalistic, bloodshot eyes of both Clinch brothers momentarily swung from Bates to Longarm, then drunkenly flicked back and forth from one lawman to the other. The sun had been up for nigh on four hours and Longarm shook his head in wonder that either of the men could stand.

"So, what's 'at to us?" Boggs snapped and fingered the buckle of his pistol belt.

"Yeah, who gives a runny shit if you two bastards are star-wearin' assholes?" Honas sneered, then let out an odd, high-pitched, almost girlish-sounding giggle.

"Both of you men are drunk and disorderly. Been a number of complaints about your conduct from local citizens."

"Complaints?" Honas grumped. "What kinda complaints? We ain't heard no complaints. Show me who's complainin', by God. They won't be complainin' fer long."

"Lady who runs the blacksmith and stable operation down the street says one a you boys insulted and abused her and spoke to her in a derogatory, filthy-mouthed manner."

Honas Clinch snorted. "I never laid a finger on that sweet-lookin' piece a fluff. An' if'n the bitch says I insulted her or mistreated her, it's nothin' more'n a case of her word agin' mine, by God."

"Well, how 'bout the way you've been mistreatin' our friendly neighborhood piano player, Mr. Clinch? Saw for myself how you'd bloodied him up. Law calls that assault, my friend."

"Ain't yer fuckin' friend, lawdog," Clinch snarled.

Quincy Bates didn't miss a beat. "Gonna have to hand your weapons over, boys. Just lay 'em on the bar and we'll walk you down to the jail to a clean, well-kept cell where you can dry out. Let you back on the street when you're sober and a bit more more civilized."

"Damned if we will," Honas Clinch sneered.

"Gonna have to take my pistols outta my cold, dead hand, you son of a bitch," Boggs added, then let out another strange, weirdly feminine giggle and hunched up as though ready to draw.

Longarm leveled his big blaster on Boggs Clinch's crotch and cocked it. In the eerie quiet that had descended on the Rusty Pump, the hammers of the massive weapon going back sounded like someone cracking walnuts with a ball-peen hammer inside a galvanized bucket.

"Well, that can be arranged, you stupid pile a walkin' shit," Longarm snapped. "Go for either one a them sidearms you've been pawin' around at and I'll cut you in half, right below your belt buckle. Shotgun at this range should turn your privates into nothin' more'n a mess of rendered flesh and bloody spray."

Boggs Clinch's peculiar, crooked, drunken smile bled off his twisted, heavily scarred face. He shot his droopy-eyed brother a nervous glance as though expecting a decision over which he had no control.

Quincy Bates brought his shotgun to bear on Honas Clinch, then smiled. "Appears you're the man who gets to make a decision today, mister. Go on ahead, you stupid son of a bitch. Get that smoke wagon on your hip a-workin'. But be warned—you touch them oiled walnut grips and one second later there won't be enough of your hand left to pick your own nose with."

Longarm added, "Both you boys are well-known for bein' about as smart as a wagonload of rocks. But the way I've got it figured, you can't be dumber'n snubbin' posts and whiskey weary to the point of makin' the mistake of drawin' down on men pointin' cocked shotguns at your guts. Now do what Marshal Bates said. Slip those pistol belts off and lay 'em on the bar. Put your hands in the air and head on down the street to the jail. You boys are gonna spend a little time in Devils River's incredibly neat *juzgado*. Either that, or you're both gonna die right here, right now. Which is it?"

Longarm silently counted to five, then raised his

weapon so that it was very obviously pointed at Boggs Clinch's fist-sized nose.

Honas lifted upturned hands in supplication and said, "Alright, alright. Let's all just calm down, gents." After a moment's silence, he unbuckled a pair of pistol belts that had four guns hanging from them, held the arsenal aloft, then added, "Think we'd best shuck 'em, Booger."

"We can take 'em, brother. Know we can."

"No, we can't. These men are killers. 'Specially that 'un over at the end of the bar. Don't do what they say, we'll end up worm bait and gettin' put in the ground tomorrow. Now do as I say and shed your pistols."

Boggs Clinch shook like a chained bear, but finally loosed his pistols, threw them onto the bar, raised his hands, then took a step away from the pile of weapons. Honas eased over to the bar, laid his cache of firearms out, then moved to his brother's side.

His shotgun still trained on the brigands, Quincy Bates said, "Got any a them teensy little irritatin' hideout guns, knives, bludgeons, or other instruments of death-dealing destruction on your persons? If so, you'd best give 'em up now. I find out you're carryin' something else, or if you try to use one of 'em, I'll kill both of you deader'n a pair a rotten fence posts."

The Clinch boys glanced at each other, then turned to the bar and unloaded another pile of small, short-barreled pistols, several knives, and a pair of leather-covered slabs of lead guaranteed to turn a man's lights out with one tap.

"That it?" Quincy snapped.

Honas tapped his brother with his elbow and motioned toward the pile. Boggs shook his head and grunted. Honas elbowed Boggs again, harder. Boggs snatched his hat off, fumbled around in the tall crown, and came out with a single-shot Remington derringer.

"Damn well best be tellin' the truth, boys," Quincy said. "I've got a jailer workin' for me who'll blow you outta your boots if you even think about tryin' to break outta one a his cells."

"Swear 'fore bleedin' Jesus," Honas whined, "that's the whole lot. Ain't nothin' left."

Bates shot a quick glance toward Longarm, who nodded and said, "Okay, fellers, just stroll on over this way, turn right on the boardwalk, and head for the jail. Keep your hands above your heads where I can see 'em."

As Honas Clinch passed Longarm, he said, "You skinned us, Marshal. No doubt about it. But when our boss, Kermit Lasher, finds out what you've gone and done, well, that's when you're gonna wish you'd a left us to our drinkin' and fun."

"Yeah, yeah, yeah. I know, Clinch. That's what I keep hearin' from all a your sort. Somebody'll get me for makin' you pay. Just shut the hell up and march your big dumb ass on down to the jail."

Clinch made out like he'd been hurt. "Ain't no need to be insultin', Marshal. Hell, we're just meeker'n a couple a little lambs now. Just like in them kids' nursery rhymes."

Longarm threw his head back and let out a rude-sounding guffaw. "Yeah, and I'm the king of France, you lyin' skunk. Shut the hell up and march."

Chapter 11

Less than an hour after Longarm and Marshal Quincy Bates snapped the locks on the Clinch brothers' separate cell doors, someone knocked at the front entrance of the jailhouse.

Bates set his coffee cup on the desk and said, "Damn. Ain't often folks 'round here bother to announce their arrival 'fore enterin' my office. Wonder who it is."

Longarm hopped out of the gregarious marshal's leather guest chair, strode to the door, and snatched it open. A toothy smile flashed across his face as he tipped his hat and said, "Well, well, well. Miss Ardella Lasher, I do believe. Nice of you to stop by, ma'am."

Shoulders back, like a lifelong Yankee drill instructor, Ardella Lasher strode into the room as though she owned the entire building and the rest of Devils River as well. Dolphus Lasher's younger sister bore not a single iota of resemblance to her more than worthless brother. Tall, rangy, and angular in almost every aspect, the blue-eyed, blond-haired, ruby-lipped gal filled out a split-crotched leather riding skirt about as well as any woman Longarm had ever seen. Appeared to Longarm that she'd pulled the garment over her beautifully shaped naked ass, sat in a

103

tub of warm water till the leather was saturated, then let it shrink-dry to fit her gorgeous behind like a second skin.

A bead of sweat ran down Longarm's temple, then traced a line to the edge of his jaw. *Jesus*, he thought. *She's got the kinda body that'd make a grown man wanna slap the hell outta his poor ole grandma.*

A tight, long-sleeved bleached muslin man's shirt, open to a near obscene level, could barely contain a pair of melon-sized breasts restrained by little more than the buttons on her brocaded silk vest. Silver-studded cowboy cuffs, a pair of tight roper gloves, and a man's flat-brimmed Stetson topped off an outfit accentuated by a set of flashy, ivory-gripped Colt Lightning pistols.

The strutting girl carried a silver-headed, braided leather quirt in one hand and slapped it against a shapely leg that dove into one of a pair of stovepipe, high-heeled boots done in green leather with fancy, lifelike eagles stitched across their fronts. Heavy Mexican rowels, the size of twenty-dollar double eagles, clinked and jingled as she swaggered into the room. A perceptible aura of tension, sexual and otherwise, surrounded the eye-catching woman like a roiling, electricity-laced thundercloud.

Quincy Bates shot to his feet and almost stumbled all over himself getting around the desk to shake the remarkable girl's hand. During the greeting he couldn't help but try and surreptitiously stare down her open-throated shirt at the amazing expanse of bosom she had on display.

No doubt about it, Longarm thought, *this girl knows what she's got and can work a man like a good cutting horse works poor, dumb, range-crazed steers.*

Eyes near bulging in their sockets, and an idiotic grin painted on his face, Bates held the Lasher woman's hand as though he had a grip on something delicately fragile that might shatter like glass, and said, "Most pleased you came by, miss. We'd heard you and your father were in town."

Ardella Lasher extracted her hand as though she'd somehow managed to pick up a rattlesnake. "Pap sent me over to post bail for our good friends the Clinch brothers. Just name the amount, Marshal, and I'll pay in cash."

Bates continued to smile like an idiot, but moved back behind his desk in a none-too-subtle effort to put the girl in her place and to appear more official. He tapped the top of the desk with one finger, then said, "Sorry, miss, but there ain't no bail been set on those particular gents. Figure they'll just have to sit in a cell till they sober up some."

Longarm pushed the door closed, suppressed a creeping grin, then leaned back against the portal, fired a fresh cheroot, and watched the unfolding entertainment.

The Lasher girl stepped up to Quincy's desk and slapped it with the business end of her quirt. "What the hell are you workin' at here, Marshal? Mind explaining why no bail has been set for our friends? I'd like to be able to explain such idiotic nonsense to my father in a way that'll keep him from comin' over here and rippin' your ears off."

An ironic grin flitted across the corners of Bates's mouth. "Well, miss, truth is we don't have a judge in Devils River at the moment. Have to wait for a circuit-ridin' adjudicator to come around from over in Uvalde. That won't be for another three weeks or so. Our local justice of the peace would usually set bond amounts for me, but he's out of town at the moment. Had to travel up to Fort Worth for a funeral."

The Lasher woman gritted her teeth and shot a hot-eyed glance over at Longarm. An ever-so-slight smile crinkled her full, pouty lips before she jerked away from his gaze. *Girl's having fun with this,* he mused.

Bates scratched his chin and looked lost in thought for

a moment. "'Course, suppose I could set the amount of a fine myself and just let 'em loose on my own," he said.

"Sounds just dandy to me. Don't much care how Honas and Boggs get turned out. How much of a fine are we talking about?" the girl snapped.

"Oh, somewhere around five hundred, I'd imagine."

Ardella Lasher took a step backward as though she'd been slapped. "Five hundred dollars?"

"Each."

"Each? For the love of sweet bleedin' Jesus, what'd they do? Kill your wife?"

"Why, no, of course not. First off, I ain't married. And second, a killin' would cost you at least two thousand apiece."

The woman threw Longarm a pleading glance as though she might be looking for help. His grinning shrug turned her back to Marshal Bates. "Well, if we don't pay the fine, when do you figure Honas and Boggs'll finally get cut loose?"

"Oh, probably sometime late tomorrow. Maybe the next day. Not sure. When you think about it, that's really not much of a stretch in jail for public drunkenness, threatening the lives of law enforcement officers, and wanton assault perpetrated on two of our most prominent citizens."

Ardella Lasher's face, along with the deep, expansive crease of her heaving bosom and the back of her graceful neck, had turned a color of red just short of purple when she snapped, "Well, then, I guess we'll just have to wait, won't we?"

"If you don't want to pay their fines, then yes, ma'am. I'd say that's about the limit of your choices."

With an aggressive slap of the quirt against a shapely leg topped by a taut, well-rounded, muscular behind, the clearly angry female made a deep-throated growling

106

sound, turned on her heel, and headed for the door. Longarm snatched his hat off, pulled the entryway open, and stood aside.

As the angry girl drew up to a spot within sniffing distance of the grinning deputy U.S. marshal, Quincy Bates called out, "You don't want to see your brother 'fore you go, miss?"

The flushed, cherry-cheeked gal tilted her head and gazed directly into Longarm's eyes as he tapped the brim of his snuff brown Stetson against his chin. The fiery aroma of raw, pulsating sex oozed off the girl. Heady, pungent fragrance was enough to give a grown man a case of the vapors. She whirled toward Bates and stomped back to his desk. The Mexican rowels clicked against the board floor like pistol shots with every angry step she took.

She pointed at the cell block door with the silver-headed quirt. "You've got my brother locked up back there, too?"

Bates eased down into the sheltering comfort of his chair, leaned back, and laced his fingers together. "Unfortunately that is most definitely the case. Indeed I do, ma'am. And he'll remain in the capable care of me and my jailor until Deputy U.S. Marshal Custis Long yonder can escort your sorry brother back to Denver for trial and suitable hanging."

Blue eyes flashed lightning bolts as Ardella Lasher drilled a sizzling, air-scorching glance back at Longarm. "Trial for what? Just what in the hell are you two badge-totin' weasels up to?" The words came out of her mouth like the snap of a ten-foot bullwhip, zipped across the room, and crackled just short of Longarm's nose.

Longarm arched an eyebrow at the girl's accusatory glare. "Why, Miss Ardella, I can't imagine that you're completely unaware of the fact that your sweet-natured, hymn-singing brother Dolphus is a wanted and dangerous man, given to rudely impetuous acts that include high crimes of a distinctly heinous nature."

Fisted hands on her hips, Ardella Lasher swelled to her full and most impressive height. She tapped an angry toe at Custis Long, curled a damp tongue over her perfect teeth, then snarled, "Wanted for what, exactly, Marshal Long?"

"He's duly and legally accused of the foul and unnatural murder of a federal judge, ma'am. Fine gent by the name of Elias Creed from over in Santa Fe, as a matter of pure fact. Seems the angelic Mr. Dolphus walked into Judge Creed's courtroom and shot the man dead."

"Well, I damn well doubt that."

"You can doubt all you like, miss, but the fact of the matter is that Dolphus is going back to Denver with me to stand trial for murder. Figure he'll very likely swing from a federal gallows for the crime. Unfortunately for him, an abundance of witnesses saw the entire sorry event."

A red-faced Ardella Lasher slapped the quirt across her palm. "Well, my pap will never allow such a monstrous thing to happen, by God."

Longarm's gaze narrowed. "Hope you'll forgive the bluntness of my next remark, miss, but Kermit's got nothing to say about the workings of federal law enforcement."

She shook the abbreviated leather whip at Longarm and snarled, "We'll just see about that, Marshal. Pap finds out 'bout Dolphus bein' locked up in this rat's nest of a jail, and I can just about promise my brother won't be a guest of the Devils River marshal's office for much longer."

Through the tiny square viewing portal of the cell block's massive entry door, Hamp Bodine yelped, "I heard that. Have you know this here ain't no 'rat's nest of a jail,' missy. Cleanest by-God lockup west of Austin." The old jailer's livid face filled the stingy opening. His voice went up an octave or more when he screeched, "And it'd be a damn sight cleaner still if'n the nasty sons a bitches we've got locked up back here'd stop pukin' on my floor, goddammit."

Ardella Lasher's head dipped, and when it came back up Longarm detected the ever-so-slight hint of a wickedly knowing smile. "Well, guess as long as I'm already here, I'll go back and speak to my brother and assure the Clinch brothers we Lashers haven't abandoned them."

Quincy Bates steepled his fingers on his stomach and said, "Be my pleasure to escort you, Miss Lasher. Just leave your pistols here on my desk."

With a grunt of exasperation, she tossed the fancy pistols onto Quincy Bates's desk, then turned toward the cell block door. "I don't need an escort. Fully capable of taking care of myself, Marshal Bates."

"Belt pistols all you're carryin'?" Quincy said.

Eyebrows knitted in a pulsating knot, the girl stopped at the still-closed cell block door, raised her arms, and slowly turned around for a full and fantastic view of her attention-grabbing body. The deliberately tantalizing move accentuated the heavy fullness of her breasts. The clingy leather riding outfit revealed virtually every crease, curve, and wrinkle, and perhaps even a tiny mole or two. The moist slit that divided the fist-sized lump behind the garment at the juncture of her shapely thighs proved so blatantly apparent as to make it appear that she had on little or nothing at all underneath.

"You see anything else on me, Marshal?" she barked.

Longarm coughed, covered his mouth with one hand and his inflamed crotch with his hat, then danced from foot to foot and coughed again to cover his suppressed amusement.

Quincy Bates eyeballed the girl's startling shape as

though caressing every curve, bulge, and indentation with his gaze, hacked a cough into one hand, then mumbled, "Uh-h-h, well, uh-h-h, no ma'am. Guess not. No detectable firearm-type weapons, at any rate."

She threw a quick, clearly challenging glance at each man, then zeroed back in on Longarm. "Either of you wanna search me?"

Bates appeared surprised by the question. "Uh-h-h, well, now that's a whole other . . . No. No, Miss Lasher. That shouldn't be necessary. No. Not at all."

Ardella lowered her arms, straightened the vest, smoothed the wrinkles over her well-rounded, muscular, saddle-toughened caboose, then said, "I'd appreciate it if you'd tell that idiot inside the jail to open the damned door."

"Heard that, too, missy," Hamp Bodine yelled. "Only idiots back here are locked up in three separate cells. Not sure which 'uns the biggest idiot of all, though. Be a tough call if'n I 'uz takin' bets. But your brother's givin' these other two mo-rons a run fer their money in the idiot race."

"Let 'er in, Hamp," Quincy yelled.

The bolt thumped on the back side of the heavy door. Bodine jerked the thick wood-and-iron slab aside, then waddled his one-legged way out of the angry girl's path as she stomped past him.

"I'd like to be left alone with my brother, if you don't mind," she said as she passed the cantankerous jailor.

Bodine leaned into the office and hooked a thumb to-ward the cells. "Okay if I leave 'er back here alone, Quince?"

"'S fine, Hamp. Let 'er have some privacy with her kin."

Bodine lumbered into the office, headed for the coffeepot, poured himself a fresh cup of belly wash, then flopped onto one of the chairs beside the chess table.

Longarm turned away from the action and fanned his face with his hat. Even with his back to the open jailhouse door, he could hear the muffled tones of Ardella Lasher and her idiot brother talking. At one point the cadence of their speech quickened and the discussion sounded as though it had turned into a bitter argument.

Longarm stuffed the hat back on his damp head, then ambled over to Quincy Bates's desk. Bates watched as the inquisitive deputy U.S. marshal picked up one of Ardella Lasher's fancy pistols, flipped the loading gate open, and rolled the cylinder. Every chamber of the scroll-engraved weapon contained a fresh .38-caliber round.

"Girl goes fully loaded," Longarm muttered, "must be figuring on trouble, Quince." He placed the pistol back on the desk as closely to the way she'd left it as he could, lit a fresh cheroot, and then resumed his spot by the front door.

Longarm cocked a concentrated ear toward the cell block and heard snatches of the conversation in the jail but couldn't make out exactly what was being said. After some minutes of heated discussion that had all the sound and passion of a nasty argument, the exchange between Ardella Lasher and her bone-headed brother fell away to a hushed level that proved nigh impossible to hear at all. Before she vacated the cell block, Longarm heard her briefly speak with each of the Clinch brothers in turn. Then she strutted back into the marshal's office, snatched up her weapons, and reholstered them.

"Believe me when I tell you this, boys, you ain't heard the last of this mess. Best hit your knees and pray to whatever god you hold dearest that we can control Obie once he finds out you've got Dolphus locked up in here.

Obie's like a big ole dog. Totally devoted to Dolphus. He finds out his master's locked up in one of these cells, there's no way to predict how he'll react. Sure, Pap'll try, but I can't guarantee anything."

Quincy Bates didn't take the angry challenge well. From behind a curling sneer, he said, "Before you leave, Miss Lasher, there is one more thing I need you to convey to your father for me."

Ardella eyed the fuming lawman with a degree of suspicion, but said, "And what might that be, Marshal?"

"Please tell ole Kermit that the Army's payroll shipment won't be coming through Devils River on Monday, or for anytime in the foreseeable future. Appears your family made a trip all the way out here to Satan's front doorstep for nothin'. Bank's got about as much money in it as an organ-grinder's tin cup."

Tight-lipped and almost scarlet in the face, Dolphus Lasher's beautiful sister shot both lawmen a hot glance, stomped her way to the front entrance, jerked it open, and slammed it behind her as she left. The swinging door hit the frame so hard a cloud of pale, gritty dust shot up from the floor and puffed across the room. The level of tension in the jailhouse suddenly drained away like rainwater running off a tin roof.

Longarm ducked his head and covered the grin on his lips with one hand. Tight-assed gal might've been mad enough to bite a chunk out of the head of a double-bit ax, but for just a second before she slammed the door, he'd caught her staring at his crotch.

Chapter 12

Longarm flopped into Quincy Bates's leather guest chair, pushed his hat to the back of his head with one finger, then said, "Don't know if it was that great an idea to tell the girl about the payroll not comin' through town, Quince."

"Aw, hell, what can it matter, Custis? They'd a found out sooner or later anyway. Bet that idiot Dolphus done already told her how he went an' spilt his guts to us. Most likely that's why they were a-yammerin' at each other so hot and heavy back yonder in the cell block just now. Goes a long way to explainin' why she had her hackles up and got flamin' mad so quick, too."

Custis Long scratched the back of a tight-muscled neck, twisted his head as though he had a brain buster of a headache coming on, then said, "Well, the Lasher bunch had two separate problems to worry over before you told Ardella that the money ain't coming—pullin' the robbery off and what to do about Dolphus, once they found out about him bein' locked up, of course."

"Sounds right to me."

"Now the one and only thing ole Kermit has to worry hisself over, Quince, is what to do about gettin' Dolphus and the Clinch brothers runnin' loose again. Kinda sharpens the focus of their attention and decision-makin' processes a bit, don't you think?"

"Uh-h-h, well, shit. Suppose maybe you might be right, Custis. Gal pissed me off. Guess I didn't put much thought into what I said to her."

"Guess not. Thing we've gotta be more'n a bit concerned 'bout right now is what to do with the Clinch brothers."

"Be happier'n a two-tailed puppy to hear any opinions you harbor on the subject, Custis."

For several seconds Longarm stared at the jail's strangely fancy tin ceiling and scratched his chin. "Truth is, Quince, can't keep the Clinch brothers locked away back there indefinitely. There are some troublesome legalities we have to consider. They got drunk, roughed up a piano player, and one of 'em—probably Honas—pawed around some on Bell Harvey. Don't amount to very much when you get to really looking at it. Be hard to legally justify a stay of more'n a few days in the hoosegow for either one of 'em. Right thing to do is fine 'em and turn 'em loose."

Quincy Bates nodded, then said, "Sounds fine to me, up to a point, that is. Cain't quite let the business of Bell's gettin' roughed up pass. Honas needs to get his ass in a really narrow crack over that 'un."

"True, but sometimes you just have to do what's best all the way around. Try to keep 'em in here, ole Kermit just might burn this place to the ground. Might do it anyway if he can't have Dolphus, too."

"That puts us back to the original question: Whaddaya think we should do?"

Longarm pulled a cheroot from his jacket pocket, tapped the end against the heel of his boot, then used the smoke to poke at the air for emphasis when he said, "Figure tomorrow, next day at the latest, you'll have to let the Clinch boys loose. Soon as they hit the street, our problems keeping Dolphus behind bars will start in earnest."

"So?"

"So, we're gonna need another gun—or maybe two if'n we can find 'em—around here helpin' out. You mentioned earlier as how you thought maybe there's at least one person left in town you could call on to lend a hand."

"Yeah, yeah, I remember that."

"Appears we're gonna need whatever assistance we can scare up, Quince. We can't all stay here in the jail till the Lasher bunch realize they ain't gettin' Dolphus back and leave town. So, you might wanna contact your man, whoever he is, and get him over here sometime today."

"Sure 'nuff said as how I might know someone. Yes I did. Tell ya, Custis, I 'uz thinkin' of askin' a feller name a Emmit Callahan to help, if we should actually need anyone."

"Callahan?"

Bates broke into a big grin. "Yep. Folk 'round here call 'im Mad Dog Emmit Callahan."

"Sweet merciful Father," Hamp Bodine hissed over his fresh cup of steaming coffee from his seat at the chess table. "You ain't thinkin' a bringin' that loco son of a bitch into this, are you?"

"Might be the only help available to us, Hamp. We may have to button the jailhouse up tighter'n Dick's hat band 'fore this whole dance shakes out. Still gonna need to patrol the town on a regular basis, and conduct all our regular duties same as ever. Extra man could give all of us some much needed relief when required. 'Specially you. 'Sides, he ain't as crazy as folks think."

Bodine looked like a man in some sort of physical

misery. "Understand all that and realize there ain't many dependable sorts left in Devils River to choose from these days. But Christ on a crutch, Quince, everyone within a hundred miles of here knows that ole Mad Dog slipped more'n one cog in his thinker mechanism back when he did all that Injun fightin' out in New Mexico and Arizona. Way I heard the tale he jus' went crazier'n a sun-stroked lizard 'cause a the mountain of poor dead folks he'd seen over all them years. 'Specially all them as died in the Antelope Mountain Massacre."

"Look, I'll admit Emmit does sometimes act a bit shy in the hat size, but when the chips are down, I'd bet everything I've got that he'll fight beside us when no one else around town will. 'Sides, if'n I'd a been at Antelope Mountain, might be nuttier'n a sack full a soft-shell pecans myself."

"Jesus," Longarm muttered. "Just how crazy is this Mad Dog Callahan, Quince?"

Bodine snorted and shook his head. "Couple a years back the moonstruck sunuvabitch blew up a cow."

Longarm glared at Bodine, squinted, and said, "Did I just hear you right? You said this upright, stellar citizen, the man Marshal Bates wants to deputize and have help us with the Lasher bunch, once blew up a cow?"

Bodine flashed a sheepish grin and nodded. "Heard me right, Marshal Long. Got into it with a feller what used to have a piece a land out on the east side of town, not far from Emmit's place. Gent by the name of Ellis Brinson. The pair of 'em went at each other ever time they crossed paths for nigh on two years. Never really got too violent. Mostly a lot of jaw jackin' and such. Just couldn't seem to be around one another 'thout gettin' into a cuss fight."

Quincy Bates twirled his coffee cup around in a wet spot on top of the desk as he said, "Then late one afternoon a year or so ago, just 'fore dark, as Ellis Brinson told it, he walked out on his porch to take in a particularly noteworthy sunset. Said a purebred Hereford cow, which he'd just purchased for some breedin' experiments he wanted to try, wandered up in the grass-poor yard between his house and barn. He'd just taken a puff off'n a hand-rolled when the cow exploded. Said he damn near choked to death."

Bodine let out a nervous giggle. "Teeth, hair, guts 'n innards of all sorts, eyeballs 'n everthang rained down all over the fuckin' place. Found the poor critter's head on the roof. Feet was all standin' right around a smokin' burnt spot where the cow exploded. Brinson swore it 'uz the most unnervin' thing he'd ever witnessed. Scared hell outta his wife 'n kids. Quince told 'im we'd do what we could. Appears he couldn't wait. Man sold out 'n left for parts unknown not long after that rather singular exploding' bovine event."

For a moment Longarm stared heavenward as though seeking divine intervention. "And Mr. Brinson believed that Callahan was responsible for the act?"

Bodine and Bates exchanged knowing glances, then Bates said, "Well, way I figured it, Custis, no one else in town 'cept ole Mad Dog woulda been nervy enough to strap dynamite to a Hereford cow and blow 'er up. Ain't that right, Hamp?"

Bodine gave his shaggy head a vigorous nod. "Damned right. 'Sides, once we confronted ole Mad Dog 'bout the fiery incident, he admitted to the crime but pointed out as how we'd never prove it."

Longarm scratched his chin, let out an exasperated sigh, then said, "Why's he runnin' loose? Sounds to me like the man oughta be sittin' in prison, or maybe in the loony bin of some asylum for the criminally insane."

Quincy Bates flashed a big grin. "Oh, he ain't that crazy. Or maybe he's just crazy like a fox. That explodin' cow trick clearly scared the bejabberous hell outta ole Brinson. Lotta other folks, too. Brinson and his whole family were so scared, they vanished in the night like a buncha travelin' gypsies. Never came back. Hard to prosecute Mad Dog for blowin' up a cow if his accuser's nowhere to be found."

Longarm stared at the ceiling for almost a minute, then picked at a hangnail before he said, "What about the bank's guards?"

"What guards?"

"Well, when I arrived in town, I noticed that the bank has no windows. It sports gun ports all around both levels of the building. Aren't there bank guards for the big-time money shipments stored there?"

"No guards at the bank, Custis," Quincy growled. "Only two employees left over there right now. Armed guards always come in on the coach. Take up their stations at those gun ports only while the shipment is in town. No help there. But Emmit Callahan owes me, and if I have to depend on a single man to help, it'd be him."

"Owes you?"

"Yes, and if I ask, he'll do anything in his power to come to my aid."

"And what exactly does he owe you for, Quince?" Longarm asked.

"I'm the man who found the skunk who raped and murdered Emmit Callahan's wife several years back. He was up in Fort Worth at the time. Some kinda business. Felt the lady would be safe out there on his property, bein' so remote and all. Saddle bum came by, saw his chance, and took it. Friend of Mrs. Callahan found the lady's body within hours of the killin'. By the time Emmit got back home, I'd run down the murderin' son of a bitch over in the Glass Mountains and killed the hell outta him."

Longarm shook his head in disbelief. "Well, can you get Emmit Callahan in here 'fore it gets dark?"

Quincy Bates hopped out of his chair, snatched a hat off the desktop, stuffed it on his head, then said, "We can go out after 'im right now. He don't live but four or five miles outside town. Got a place right at the base of a pile a rocks not far out on the east side a town. We can ride out, tell 'im what we want, and bring 'im back with us. How's that sound?"

"Works for me. Quicker we get the deal done, the better," Longarm said as he rose and moved toward the door with Quincy hot on his heels.

Longarm's hand had barely touched the polished brass knob when a head-scratching Hamp Bodine said, "Reckon Emmit'll wanna bring the Beast along if'n he comes."

Longarm stopped in the doorway, cast a squint-eyed, puzzled look back into the office, then said, "The Beast?"

Bodine shook his head, "Yeah, that's what he calls his dog. 'Course ain't no one 'round Devils River that's real sure the creature's all dog. Damned thing looks like a cross 'tween a timber wolf and a grizzly bear. Might be a dog, but if so, it's the biggest 'un me or anybody else 'round here done ever seen."

As if to reassure his newly made friend, Quincy Bates reached out and touched Longarm on the elbow, then snatched his hand back and waved Bodine's comment away like an annoying insect. "Aw hell, ole Mad Dog's animal ain't never hurt no one 'round here. Not yet, anyway."

"While that's true," Bodine said, "sure as hell wouldn't want the hairy sunuvabitch after me. 'Course they's plenty a tall tales, rumors, and downright lies bein' told 'bout how many folks that monster's done rubbed out somewhere, sometime."

"We'll worry 'bout the Beast, if we must, when the time comes," Bates said, and pushed Longarm on through the doorway.

As the two lawmen stepped onto the boardwalk, Bates called over his shoulder, "Button 'er up tight, Hamp. Don't let anyone in till we get back. And I mean anyone, you understand?"

The thick bolt crunched into place behind them. Through the thick wooden panel, Bodine yelled, "Don't be a-worryin', Quince. Won't open 'er up again till I can see your ugly face in this here stingy little winder."

Longarm tugged on Bates's sleeve and said, "Any way to get from here down to Bell's place without everyone in town, especially the Lasher bunch, seein' us?"

Twisting waves of heat rose from the baked street as Quincy Bates pointed to an alleyway between Godwin's Meat Market and the Texas State Land Office. "It'll just about double the distance of our walk, but we can get behind them buildings on the north side a the street through that alley yonder. Can't see nothin' back there from the Cattleman's. Make our way to the west end, somewhere down 'round the Ice House, then we can cross back over. Pick up the horses and go out through the rear entrance of Bell's place. Make our way east behind everything on this side a the street. Nobody in town will even notice we're gone till we get back."

"Okay," Longarm grunted. "Let's do it."

The quickly formulated ruse turned into a hot, strenuous hike, and by the time they'd made it to Bell Harvey's stable, both men were drenched in sweat. Longarm stepped into the shaded, cooler inner depths of the barn, whipped a bandana from his hip pocket, then mopped his dripping face and brow.

"God, it's hotter'n a fresh-forged horseshoe out there," Longarm said as he doffed his hat and wiped the saturated leather band inside. "Little nothin' of a walk and it feels like blisters are popping out on my boot heels."

Glistening with sweat, her striking face smeared with streaks of something black, Bell Harvey strode from an empty stall carrying a pitchfork. A mischievous smile danced across her lips when she leaned against one of the end posts, played with the front of her shirt, glanced from one man to the other, then said, "Well, well, well. Ain't often I get two gentlemen callers sniffin' 'round down here at the same time."

All business, Quincy Bates said, "No time for female folderol, Bell. Need two horses. If Ole Blue's not out, I'll take him. Gotta make a quick visit out on the east side of town."

Longarm threw the girl a barely perceptible shake of the head, then said, "Figure the bangtail I rode in on is still restin' up. If you've got somethin' else I could take out, I'd appreciate it, Miss Harvey."

She motioned toward the back of the barn. "Right this way, Marshal Long. Blue roan a yours could do with another day or so of rest. Got a blood bay mare back here in the stall on the far side of your animal that I think'll work just fine." As she strutted ahead of Longarm, she called over her shoulder, "Ole Blue's in his usual spot 'bout halfway down over yonder on the other side, Quince. Sure he'll be more'n glad to see you."

Longarm retrieved his own saddle from the stall rails between his animal and Bell's blood bay mare. As he threw the rented California rig over the shiny-coated animal's back, the randy woman slipped up behind him in the tight, dark cubicle, ran a hand down between his legs, and gave his always-up-for-any-kind-of-action love muscle a tender but insistent squeeze and caress.

"No time for fun and games right now, Bell," he said, then bent over and reached under the mare for the cinch strap. The awkward move forced her hand away from his awakening prong.

As he worked to get the saddle fitted properly, Bell encircled his waist with both arms, pressed her rock-hard breasts to his back, and rubbed her crotch against him. The smell of her sex invaded his nostrils and overpowered everything else in the stable. "We had such a good time last night, just thought you might want a second helpin'," she breathed into one ear.

"No doubt about that, darlin'. Would dearly love to give you another ass-burnin' ride, but not right here and not right now." He untangled himself from her eager, grasping clutches and went to work fitting the bay with a horsehair bridle and curb bit. "Hell, girl, you gotta get a grip. Quincy ain't no more'n thirty feet away."

Bell grabbed at his crotch again, then hissed, "Know we can't do the whole dance, but you can pull it out and let me nibble on it a little. Please, Custis," she moaned into his ear and squeezed his rapidly stiffening trouser snake with considerably more enthusiasm. "Oh, God, the big devil's wakin' up, ain't he?" she whispered.

He threw the reins over the bay's head, then backed the animal out. Once into the wider open area of the stable, Longarm shot a quick look over the saddle and into the dark corner he'd just vacated. Devils River's sultry blacksmith had loosed the tie to her leather apron's top and opened her shirt.

With a stiff-nippled breast in each hand, Bell Harvey cast a heavy-lidded, lust-laden glance at the object of her unrestrained desire, then pushed both beautiful boobs upward. "Come on, big boy. Come and get it," she hissed.

Her incredibly long, snaky tongue flicked out at the tip of one erect, flint-tipped nipple. An overheated gaze never left Longarm as she sucked the stiff, thumb-sized bit of flesh into her mouth, let it out with a loud, wet, sloppy *pop*, and then quickly switched to the other nipple.

Noise from Quincy's end of the stable jerked Longarm's gaze away from Bell's blatantly carnal actions. The town's marshal had his animal ready and was moving Longarm's direction. A quick glance back into the darkness revealed that Bell Harvey had somehow managed to vanish like a beautiful, horny ghost.

Good God, Longarm thought, *the randy gal's really something, but I gotta focus my mind on Kermit Lasher and how to keep the man in check, not Bell Harvey's steamin' snatch.* No doubt the wild-assed gal could turn a man's head, but the second problem could easily get him killed if he didn't pay attention.

Chapter 13

Longarm led the rented blood bay through the stable's rear entrance and into Bell Harvey's empty corral, stepped into a stirrup, threw a leg over the horse, and settled in for a long, hot ride. He followed Quincy Bates through a jumble of houses, shacks, jacales, tents, barns, and outbuildings—many abandoned—that littered the rough, baking landscape for several blocks behind all the businesses on the south side of Devils River's main thoroughfare. Wiry yellow-toothed dogs skulked beneath rickety porches or behind any sheltering cover available. Most snarled and yapped at the men as they passed.

Here and there a pinch-faced woman peeked from the doorway or curtained window of one of the tired, weather-blasted houses, but no children seemed in evidence anywhere. For the first time Longarm realized that he'd noticed no schoolhouse on the main thoroughfare or amongst the hodgepodge of dilapidated homes. Perhaps the town located theirs in some area he'd not yet seen. That had to be the way of things.

The going got somewhat easier once the lawmen had picked their way through the muddled collection of Devils River's occupied and unoccupied homes and back to the coarse, rutted stage road running east. Longarm knew the raised, man-made roadbed would carve a long, bleak, relentless path south and east past Kelly Peak, Boiling Mountain, and Turkey Mountain into Uvalde, and then march inexorably on toward San Antonio.

The harsh, rolling countryside in every direction for as far as the eye could see was home to nothing but armadillos, coyotes, scorpions, possums, and tarantulas. Nearly treeless, decorated by an unforgiving nature with short, stubby, twisted brush and rare patches of tough, bunched grass, the remorseless landscape had the power to intimidate even the most audacious and skilled of travelers.

Barely an hour into the ride, Quincy Bates pointed to a rugged outcropping of rocks north of their position and said, "Gotta turn off the road not too far up ahead. Trail leads from the road up to Emmit's place."

"Say he lives at the base of that heap a rocks?"

"Yeah. Official get-it-off-the-map name for the spot is Dry Devil's Peak. But most folks 'round here call it the Log Pile. Emmit came to town several years ago and bought a pissant-sized horse operation up there. Not sure how much horse raisin' he really does, though. Mostly I think the man does his best just to live from day to day and tries real hard to be left the hell alone."

Longarm gauged the Log Pile two or three miles off the Uvalde road. Every hundred yards or so along that entire distance a new sign grew out of the hard-baked ground like the misshapen act of a perverted temperament. Broken, sun-bleached planks attached to twisted, weather-desiccated tree limbs jammed in the ground, and held up by piles of rocks, announced the author's displeasure at having anyone invade his privacy.

First marker Longarm noticed was emblazoned in bloodred paint with rude lettering that warned the reader to GO BACK NOW. THIS IS PRIVATE PROPERTY. Succeeding messages got more stringent the closer unwanted visitors came to Emmit Callahan's isolated ranch house. Mounds of animal bones decorated the rocky base of each of the sun-shriveled stalks used to hold the dire warnings in place. Last sign simply read TRESPASSERS WILL BE SHOT DEAD—THEN FED TO HUNGRY PIGS.

Quincy led the way through the only opening in a primitive rail fence surrounding the main ranch building. Appeared to Longarm that the tumbled-down enclosure was comprised of the same kind of emaciated timbers used to display Callahan's gruesomely threatening admonitions to stay the hell away. A sign over the crude gate announced the place as the DEVIL'S DEN.

Dozens of chickens and guinea hens, several cats, a number of scrawny turkeys, a host of wild, squealing pigs, and at least one peacock scattered for safety as the lawmen urged their horses across the grassless yard. They eased their sweat-drenched animals as near to the front porch of Callahan's crude ranch building as possible, then reined up.

Typical of most dog-run, South Texas habitations, the whole clapboard-sided shebang sat atop wooden piers that raised the three-part structure approximately two feet off the ground. The resulting open space beneath the home allowed for much-needed air to circulate, but, unfortunately, also permitted access by any animal—tame, wild, or otherwise—in search of relief from the heat. It was obvious to Longarm that a woman had surely once lived in the house, for the wispy remnants of stylish curtains still hung in the windows and wildflowers grew in jumbled profusion along each end of the rough building.

The elevated kitchen occupied a single room on one side of a wide, breeze-catching, open porch that had also once served as a dining area. The room on the opposite side of the exposed deck was typically used as the inhabitant's sleeping quarters. Wisps of cook smoke trailed from a galvanized pipe that jutted from the roof of the kitchen area. The pungent aroma of fresh-cooked coffee wafted across the porch and tickled the edges of Longarm's nose.

The roof, covered in split cedar shingles, had aged from reddish orange to a soft, silvery gray color. The deep, shaded center veranda sported a rugged table, a number of worn, straight-backed, cane-bottomed chairs, and what looked like the shattered remnants of a dilapidated couch.

A massive, droop-jawed hound had draped its hairy, flop-eared self atop the ruined settee, but failed to move, twitch, or even acknowledge the arrival of strangers on the property. While the biscuit eater didn't deign to voice anything like disapproval of an invasion by unfamiliar people, something unseen, within the dark recesses of the kitchen side of the house, did. A disturbing, deep-throated growl rumbled through the open, unscreened doorway. The snarl rolled like low thunder across the dried slats of the plank porch, shook the front steps, and crept down each lawman's goose bump–covered back. Icy-hot crawling sensation of being eaten alive settled at the point where each man's spine was attached to his tense, disconcerted ass.

Longarm's hand eased toward the carved-bone grips of his pistol. Quincy Bates might display the faith of the longtime converted when it came to Mad Dog Callahan, but Custis Long didn't know the man or the horrifying pet Hamp Bodine had described, and figured it best not to take any boneheaded chances.

Someone inside, with a voice that easily matched the atavistic sound the concealed animal had made, said, "No,

128

Beast, no. Down. Settle down, boy. Just some friendly visitors, looks like. Don't appear as how we'll have to kill nobody today."

Something heavy thumped to the wooden floor and caused the entire structure to vibrate as it moved from the back side of the building and made its lumbering way to the front door. Longarm couldn't believe his eyes when Emmit Callahan stooped over and stepped across the crude threshold. Nothing Hamp Bodine or Quincy Bates had said about Callahan could have prepared the surprised deputy U.S. marshal for what he beheld.

The lord of the Devil's Den bore a hand-shaking resemblance to a well-fed grizzly bear. Unshaven and sporting a head of long, carefully barbered hair and a beard to match, Emmit Callahan's immaculate and fancy attire belied his somewhat leonine facial appearance. He wore a spotless, ruffle-fronted white shirt of the type usually seen when a man saw fit to bedeck himself in the raiment of someone on his way to the local opera house. A fancy plaited, black leather bolo tie, held in place with a sterling silver slide the size of a hen egg, highlighted a wine red paisley vest buttoned over the shirt.

Cleaned and pressed gray pinstriped pants disappeared into a pair of polished knee-high cavalry boots. Gaudy Mexican spurs with rowels the size of *cincuenta-peso* gold pieces almost finished off Mad Dog Callahan's surprising appearance. But the crowning accessory to the whole bizarre outfit was a bloodred sash used to hold a brace of silver-plated Colt pistols that sported polished, solid gold grips. To Longarm, Callahan looked like a gaudy, outsized version of a photo he'd once seen of Wild Bill Hickok when the famed pistoleer was in his prime.

At Callahan's side stood a dog the size of a Shetland pony. Coarse, shaggy hair rose off the animal's back from its massive neck to the base of a tail as thick as a bull whacker's upper arm. Bared canine teeth the size of a grown man's thumb jutted from behind a curled blue-black lip. And from deep inside a chest as big as a steamer trunk, a low, rumbling growl made the hair on Longarm's neck stand to attention and vibrate like picked banjo strings.

Callahan hooked a thumb behind one pistol, then scratched the dog behind the ears with his free hand. He didn't even have to bend over to reach the monster. For the first time since their arrival, the creature stopped growling.

"Well, spit it out, Quince. What you boys doin' out here? Figure you gotta be wantin' somethin' awful bad to come all the way out to the Devil's Den. Ride past every single one a my signs between here and the Uvalde road. Sure's hell ain't lookin' for a cup a my coffee."

Quincy Bates leaned on the horn of his saddle, pushed his hat to the back of his head, then said, "Never asked before, Emmit, but I need your help. Got a situation back in town that's gonna require a man I can depend on."

"Situation?"

"Yeah, right ticklish situation."

"Could your *situation* possibly require me to kill the hell outta somebody?"

"Don't know about that for certain sure, Emmit. But, as you can well understand, there's always the possibility for just such a deadly prospect given the circumstances I now find myself confronted with."

Eyes the color of bleached slate shifted toward Longarm. As if attached to its master by unseen strings, the dog's head swiveled in the same direction at the exact same time. "Who's your friend, Quince?"

Bates motioned toward his fellow lawdog, then said, "Oh, gotta forgive my manners, Emmit. This here's Deputy U.S. Marshal Custis Long. Come to town all the way from Denver to pick up a man I just kinda by accident happen to have locked up in my jail."

Callahan's gaze jerked back to Quincy Bates. "Locked up? Who you got locked up?"

"Dolphus Lasher."

"Ole Kermit Lasher's idiot son?"

"Yep. That's the one."

"Well, I'll just kiss my own ass. So Kermit will likely be a-comin' to town to get the boy loose. That the problem?"

"No, Emmit, not exactly. At least part of your surmising did hit the mark. See, Daddy's already in town. He's only just now hearin' the news 'bout Dolphus. Way we've got it figured, Kermit's gonna want the kid turned out, and damned quick. So you were right 'bout that part."

"And I can't allow that," Longarm said. "Man's destined for a short rope and a long drop back in Denver."

An eerie, otherworldly smile oozed across Emmit Callahan's lips. "Why don't you just go on ahead and kill Dolphus? Walk back to the cell block, shoot him two or three times? Was me, that's what I'd do."

Bates nodded. "Yeah. Probably shoulda killed the worthless skunk 'stead a just bustin' him across his rock-hard noggin like I did when I took him into custody. Didn't for sure know who he was at the time. But I just can't justify cold-bloodedly murderin' the boy while he's locked up like a pet rabbit."

Callahan grunted, stared at the top of his hairy friend's head for a second, then said, "Okay. I'll help. Owe you one, Quincy, a big 'un. Told you some years back I'd be there if you ever needed me. 'Sides, if there's even the slightest chance I might have an opportunity to kill Kermit Lasher, I wouldn't pass up such a chance for any amount of money. You want me to bring Beast along?"

Bates scratched his chin, then said, "Well, I'm gonna

leave that 'un up to you, Emmit. But you know how Hamp feels about the animal. They don't seem to get along all that well. And given that the four of us could be spendin' an unknowable amount of time together, you might wanna give it some thought."

Callahan glanced down at the enormous animal by his side, then back up at Quincy Bates. "Well, Quince, Beast goes where he pleases and most of the time that's with me. Two of us are virtually inseparable. 'Sides, Beast is gettin' some on the old side. Ain't near what he used to be. Just likes to bluff a lot. So, Beast will be comin' along, and I guess ole Hamp'll just have to make do with however the situation develops."

Longarm said, "Whether the animal comes or not makes no difference to me one way or the other, Mr. Callahan. But I think we need to get back to town as soon as possible. Can you leave right now?"

A huge, toothy smile opened in Callahan's beard. "Nothin' holdin' me here 'cept pullets and cats, Marshal Long. We can head back right now. All I gotta do is get the Man Killer, a bag of shells, and saddle a horse."

"The Man Killer?" Longarm said. "Can't wait to see that, whatever it might be."

Callahan strode across his home's open porch, disappeared inside the sleeping quarters, and emerged a few seconds later carrying a short-barreled .10-gauge Greener that looked like a silver-and-gold match for his fancy pistols. A stuffed, canvas ammo bag hung from a leather strap draped over one of Callahan's thick shoulders.

Longarm eyeballed the silver-plated, gold-engraved weapon's polished, checkered walnut stock and forearm, then said, "Well, that oughta do the job. Damned intimidatin' piece of artillery."

Mad Dog Callahan gave the impressive weapon an appraising, almost loving look. "I like that, Marshal Long.

Maybe that's what I shoulda named her—the Intimidator. Yeah, I really like that. A bit less brutally factual than the Man Killer. Think I just might adopt it for my own. Yeah, the Intimidator."

Longarm tipped his hat, then said, "Weapon is a beauty, Emmit. Be right honored to have you call her something I just happened to come up with."

Little more than an hour later, with an angry, rust-colored sun sinking into the west, the trio hit the eastern edge of Devils River, the Beast trailing behind at his own pace. Longarm immediately detected more activity than he'd seen since arriving in the remote village. Groups of four and five people stood on the boardwalks in front of Zang's saloon, Katy's Café, and across the street near the empty Devils River Music Hall, at Godwin's Meat Market and Maynard's Drug Store. They cast anxious, furtive glances toward the returning lawmen, shaded their mouths with open hands, and talked low and fast.

Gawkers, gapers, and a host of other loafers with little or nothing else to do dawdled in the street and appeared to gesture toward Quincy Bates's office and jailhouse. Alarmed by what he saw, Bates, trailed by Longarm, Callahan, and the Beast, spurred his animal and raced toward the town lockup.

From fifty feet away, Longarm noted that the front facade of the squatty, fortress-like building was riddled with a surprising number of scattered, randomly placed bullet holes and that the westernmost corner of the cow country hoosegow appeared to have been set afire. God only knew what had become of Hamp Bodine, or anyone else still inside.

Chapter 14

Quincy Bates jumped from his animal's back as it came to a full, stiff-legged, crow-hopping stop. He hit the ground running, leaped onto the boardwalk, and set to hammering on the jail's thick front door with a closed fist. Many of the idlers and onlookers scattered with the appearance of heavily armed men on horseback, and soon the street was near empty again.

"Hamp," he yelled. "Hamp, you in there? Hamp, it's Quince. Answer me. Open the door, goddammit."

Longarm hopped off Bell Harvey's blood bay, pulled his Winchester from its saddle boot, and moved up behind Bates to offer cover in the event they'd all stepped into an ambush. On closer examination, he could tell that the flames had left some of the thick timbers scorched and blackened, but the blaze appeared to have either gone out on its own or been doused by someone no longer on the scene.

Flashy .10-gauge shotgun in hand, Callahan soon joined Longarm and Bates, then turned to face the street. Appearing completely unconcerned for his own personal safety, he used his immense bulk to shield both the other men.

"That you, Quince?" The question came from behind the bullet-peppered door, but sounded distant and weak.

Bates stood back a step, whacked the entrance again, then yelled, "Hell, yes, it's me, Hamp. Marshal Long and Emmit Callahan as well. Open up and let us in."

After almost a full minute of peculiar and protracted silence, Longarm heard the heavy iron bolt slide back and the jail's lead-blasted entryway creaked open. Pistol drawn, he followed Quincy Bates when the anxious marshal pushed his way inside.

Hamp Bodine hobbled to the nearest chair on a makeshift crutch, fashioned from one of the hat racks Longarm had noticed earlier. Smeared with caked blood, the old deputy's face was drawn in pain. One bloodshot, blackened eye had nearly swelled shut. A number of deep cuts decorated his damaged cheeks, ears, and lips. Bedraggled clothing hung on the man in ragged, tattered strips.

Not one piece of furniture occupied a space in the office where Longarm and Quincy had left it. Shattered chairs lay tossed about the room, or in piles of useless splinters. Overturned and broken, the corner cot's bedding was strewn about the floor amidst piles of paper displaced from the top of the marshal's desk.

Dumbfounded, hands upturned like a man seeking guidance from any heavenly presence available, Quincy Bates stood in the middle of his office and said, "Sweet merciful Father. What in the blue-eyed hell happened, Hamp? Looks like the wrath of God fell on this place."

Through a deeply split lip and chipped teeth, Bodine snapped, "Lord, I wish. Fuckin' Clinch brothers happened, that's what."

Longarm placed a comforting hand on the old man's trembling shoulder. "Exactly what do you mean by that, Hamp? What about the Clinch brothers?"

"Sons a bitches is gone, that's what, by God. Busted out. Flew the coop. Slipped the hook. Headed for parts unknown. Unknown by me, anyway."

Quincy Bates's faced twisted into a creased knot of deeply lined pain. "Gone? How?"

"Simple. Both a you badge-wearin', jackass, professional law-bringin' types musta missed the short-barreled, cloverleaf Colt House pistol ole Honas had hid on his nasty-stinkin'-assed person."

"No, we searched those boys," Longarm said. "Searched 'em good before we let you lock 'em up."

"Didn't search 'em good enough, goddammit," Bodine shot back. "'Bout fifteen minutes after you fellers left fer Emmit's place, they called me to the back a-complainin' that the one named Boggs'd come down sick or some-thin'. Hadn't even stepped 'cross the threshold of the lockup when I found the end a my nose inside the barrel of ole Honas's teensy little pissant four-popper."

"The girl. Ardella," Bates shouted, "that's where the pistol came from. Shoulda searched her shapely ass 'fore we let 'er go back there. Knew she was gonna be a hatful a trouble soon as she sashayed her twitchin' ass in here."

Propped against the frame of the open front door, Emmit Callahan said, "Well, the Clinch boys obviously didn't shoot you, Hamp. How'd you end up all beat to hell and gone?"

The Beast loped past his master and into the office. Huge dog wandered over to the corner where the cot had once sat, pawed around for a few seconds, then dropped into a heap like he'd lived there all his life.

Bodine's eyes got as big as a set of saddlebags and he groaned as though in pain. Finally tore his eyes off the animal and said, "Once 'em two bastards was outta their cells, Honas pressed that stingy little pistol's muzzle up again' the side of my head and pulled the trigger. Figured

137

I 'uz a dead 'un fer sure. Nasty little bitch of a gun misfired. So I went and slapped it outta his hand faster'n double-geared lightnin'. Lucky for me, brass-framed piece of junk landed in the only empty, locked cell we've got back yonder. Pitched the keys into the lockup with the gun. That's when the fight started."

Longarm gazed around the shattered, litter-strewn room and shook his head. "Must've been one hell of a scrap."

"Well, as Quincy can attest," Bodine huffed, "I've been known to scuffle with the best of 'em. Fought 'em in the cell block fer a spell. Fought 'em in here. Fought 'em on the floor, against the walls, on the furniture, and I'd a fought 'em like cockroaches crawlin' 'round on the ceilin' if'n I'd a had to."

"I'd a paid to see that." Callahan snorted.

Bodine ignored the remark and continued. "Got my hands on a chair and damn near beat ole Boggs to stupefied insensibility 'fore his rock-headed brother managed to wrestle me to the floor. Ole Honas kept me pinned down long enough for Boggs to recover some. That's when the pair of 'em took to kickin' hell outta me. Stomped on my poor ass till my wooden leg come loose. Then Honas grabbed the floppin' sucker, ripped it completely off, and went to beatin' on me with it. God A'mighty, he put some bumps on me."

Longarm suppressed an amused smile. "Let me get this straight. You're sayin' that Honas Clinch thumped hell outta you with your own leg?"

"Ain't funny, goddammit. Cocksucker put knots the size of goose eggs all over my head, arms, back, legs. Wooden leg a mine's tough as a spoke from a Concord coach wheel. Sunuvabitch Honas went at me like a man drivin' railroad spikes. Damn near beat me unconscious, but, praise Jesus, I recovered long enough to give about as good as I got and then chase 'em out the door. That's when they went a-runnin' off down the street. Bastards took my fuckin' leg with 'em."

Longarm looked away, toed the plank floor, then said, "Took your leg? You did just say they took your leg, didn't you?"

"Yes, by God. That's what I'm a-sayin'. Perverted bastards stole my fuckin' leg. Good thing the gun rack was locked, otherwise they'd've got themselves armed up again and killed me sure 'nuff."

Longarm strode to the doorway and acted like he was looking around Emmit Callahan and into the street. "What was Dolphus doin' during all this fightin', kickin', stompin', and leg rippin'?"

"Aw, hell, he wanted loose, too. Yelped like a kicked dog. Hollered, whined, begged, and rattled his cage like one a them hairy apes you'd see in a big city zoo. Man sounded so pitiful got me to figurin' as how he could wrench tears out'n a glass eye, for God's sake. Ain't heard nothin' much outta him lately and ain't felt like goin' back there to check on 'im, either. But, hell, he's okay, just disappointed 'cause he didn't get away with 'em others."

Quincy Bates turned his swiveling chair upright, slid it behind his battered desk, then eased into it as though he'd found heaven. He put his hands behind his head, laced his fingers together, then said, "If Ardella Lasher's the one who supplied them boys with a weapon, wonder why she didn't give that itty-bitty pistol to her brother?"

Longarm turned back into the room, then scratched his chin for a second before saying, "Stupid as Dolphus is, could be she was afraid he'd go and pick the wrong time to pull it and get himself shot to pieces."

Quincy slapped his leg. "Ha. Now that sounds way too logical for my taste."

"Then again," Longarm continued, "maybe you and me just didn't do as thorough a search job as we thought and ole Honas had the gun hid on his person somewheres the whole time, just like Hamp said. But it don't really matter how they got loose, 'cause once them boys hit the street again, you can bet that wasn't the end of the dance anyway, was it, Hamp?"

Bodine shifted in his seat as though making an attempt to find a comfortable spot for his bottomless nub. "Hell, no, 'twern't. Dragged my one-legged self over to the door and managed to get 'er closed and bolted up. No more'n ten minutes later the whole damned Lasher bunch musta showed up out there on the boardwalk and went to blastin' hell outta the front a this place."

"From the looks of the walls I'd figure on at least four, maybe five of 'em. And from all appearances every man jack of 'em went through a hatful of ammunition," Long-arm said.

Bodine shook his finger at Longarm, then turned on Bates. "Boys, swear 'fore Jesus, sounded like Chickamauga in here, for Christ's sake. Gunfire and bombardment was almost like the second comin' durin' that battle."

Emmit Callahan shook his shaggy head. "Didn't know you fought at Chickamauga, Hamp."

"Damn right. 'Member as how I had to stop killin' men long enough that day to pick me a wad a cotton so's I could plug up my ears 'cause the blastin' was so bad. Anyway, after all the hellacious shootin' from the street outside, thought I smelled smoke. That's when I got to feelin' purty sure my time was up, and I'd be shakin' hands with Jesus 'fore the sun went down. Figured to be a crispy critter for certain sure, yessir, surely did."

"Who put the fire out?" Quincy said.

"Don't got any real idea 'bout that 'un, Quince. I 'uz layin' low and prayin'. Didn't see or hear much a nothin' for a spell 'fore I got up nerve enough to open the door and sneak a peek around. By then whatever flames

140

there'd been was nothin' but a little in the way of a smol-derin' spot on the corner and the sons a bitches responsi-ble had disappeared."

Bodine's last word still dangled in the air when Elton Jackson pushed his way past Emmit Callahan, then came to a swaying stop right in the middle of the room. Nearly out of breath, he said, "Marshal, them ole boys what slapped me around down at the Rusty Pump earlier come runnin' down the street 'while ago. Busted into the Pump like wild animals. Soon's they laid eyes on me they went to hollerin' 'bout it bein' my fault they'd had to spend some time locked up. Well, I hit the back door runnin'. Didn't stop till I got to Eli Cobb's barn behind the Cattle-man's. Been hidin' under a pile a hay till just a few min-utes ago."

"You know where they are now, Mr. Jackson?" Long-arm said.

"On the way over here I ran 'cross some folks out on the street what said they'd seen 'em meet up with another evil-lookin' type or two, and the whole bunch of 'em spent near half an hour shootin' hell outta your jail. Heard the gunfire, but I 'uz too spooked to come out from under my haystack. Then I smelled smoke. Folks I talked with said as how them evil sons a bitches had torched the mar-shal's office and then headed for Bell Harvey's stable. Thought fer sure the jail'd be burnt to the ground when I got here, and all you fellers would most likely be dead."

Quincy Bates hopped to his feet, fumbled in his vest pocket, and finally came up with a key for the padlock to the gun rack behind his desk. He tossed the heavy pad-lock onto his desk, opened the gun rack, and pulled out the same pair of short-barreled shotguns he and Longarm had carried earlier that morning.

"It's still loaded," Bates said as he tossed one of the weapons to Longarm. "Think we'd best get on down to

141

Bell's place. Don't like the sound of what Elton just said one damned bit."

"Me neither," Longarm snapped.

Callahan ran his fingers through his beard, scratched his chin, then said, "Am I missin' somethin' here?"

Quincy stopped in the open doorway, turned back, and said, "Stay with Hamp, Emmit. Me and Marshal Long are gonna slip on down to Bell's and take a look around. Keep the door closed. Shoot the hell outta anyone other'n the two of us that tries to get in here."

Chapter 15

While the sun hadn't completely set, light from flickering lamps fell through the windows of businesses all along the walk down Devils River's main thoroughfare from Marshal Quincy Bates's office to Bell Harvey's stable. The dusty, rutted lane had emptied of people like spit running off a red-hot stove lid. Longarm's gaze flicked from one spot along the boardwalks to another as quickly as he could shift his eyes back and forth.

As the two lawmen slowly made their way down the middle of the street, Longarm turned to Bates and, under his breath, said, "Don't like the lay of this business one damned bit, Quince. Hell, they could be hidin' anywhere. Behind the curtains of any window facin' the street. On the roof of Davis House, or that Chinese laundry yonder. We're just a couple a sittin' ducks out here in the street like this. Should be up on the boardwalks on either side sneakin' along under the porch covers and awnings. Be a helluva lot safer."

"'S true, amigo, but we need to find out about Bell soon as possible. Ain't got time to be doin' no Comanche tiptoe and worryin' ourselves over whether somebody might take a shot at us from hidin'. One of 'em uglier'n hammered cow-shit bastards shows his face, or anything else for that matter, I'm gonna pepper the hell out 'im with this big blaster, sure as red peppers are hot and icicles are cold."

A few more steps brought the pair to a spot directly in front of Davis House. Across the street and two doors down, Longarm eyeballed the front of the Cattleman's, but didn't notice any movement. "Shit," he said, "I can't believe the big dumb sons a bitches would be stupid enough to cause Bell any more problems today."

Quincy pointed with the barrel of his weapon. "Look, Custis. There's somebody a-standin' out front of the Ice House. Big mother. Christ, he's nigh on big as Mad Dog Emmit."

"Yeah, I see 'im. Bet my two-dollar Ingersoll railroader's watch that's Obidiah Lasher."

"How can you tell?"

"'Cause, as you so rightly observed, other than a few horses at the hitch rails, he's the biggest fuckin' thing on the street right now."

Quincy's Greener made a sound like a cottonwood limb snapping when he pulled both hammers back. "Well, if he's lookin' for a fight, let's go give him one."

Longarm moved to the boardwalk while Quincy kept to the middle of the street. As they approached Young's Mercantile, two doors away from the Ice House, Quincy waved his friend to a halt.

Flickering light from the rugged saloon's plate-glass window and batwing doors trickled out onto the massive bulk of Obidiah Lasher. Piss-poor illumination revealed that the man was leaning against a porch pillar and hard at work on a hand-rolled.

"Can see you lawdogs," Obie Lasher growled. "Ain't that dark yet. Been a-watchin' you fuckers ever since you snuck past the Rusty Pump." He scratched a lucifer to life, stoked the fresh tobacco, took a deep drag, flicked the dying match into the street, then waved for them to approach. "Come on in, boys. Ain't nothin' gonna happen. Got my word on it. Pap done put the leash on the Clinch boys— leastways for a little while. And while I'd like to kill both of ya for lockin' baby brother Dolphus up, Pap says I cain't do it. Not yet, anyway."

Longarm stayed on the boardwalk and stopped near the westernmost corner of Woo's Chinese Laundry. Position put him little more than twenty feet from Ardella's bigger-than-a-Dallas-bank-building brother. He cocked his own weapon and waited. Nervy son of a bitch made a damned good target, he thought.

No quit or backup in Quincy Bates as he approached Obie from the street. When he stopped, the men could've spit on each other. "Want them Clinch boys back, mister. They broke outta my jail 'fore their time was up."

Lasher let out a rumbling snort. Derisive snicker sounded like something a man would expect to hear from a grizzly bear cornered in the back of a dead-end cave. "Well, why don't you go on ahead an' wish in one hand and shit in the other'n fer 'bout a week and see which a the two of 'em fills up first, Mr. Marshal."

Longarm glanced into the deepening darkness of the alleyway between the laundry and the watering hole, then eased up on the Ice House saloon's share of the boardwalk.

"Look," Bates snapped, "ain't about to stand out here in the street and argue with your big ass 'bout this. We're talkin' a matter of law. And far as I can see—"

Before he could finish his thought, Lasher snarled, "Fuck your law, mister. You've got a far more pressin' problem than whether you can put the Clinch boys back behind bars for slappin' some pissant piano player."

Quincy Bates took another step forward. "And just what in the hell might that be?" he said.

Lasher snatched the cigarette from angry, snarling lips, then hooked a thumb over his shoulder in the direction of the saloon's entrance at his back. "Y'all come on inside. Pap's a-waitin'. He'll explain everythang fer ya." Then he turned on a jingling heel and disappeared through the Ice House's flapping doors.

Bates and Longarm closed on the batwings at the same time. Longarm grabbed his friend by the arm, then said, "Let's give 'er a real good lookin' over 'fore we do anything rash, Quince. No point rushin' into this thing now that we've gone this far."

The antsy lawmen peered over the café-style panels and into a cramped, narrow room. To their right, no more than two or three steps across the rugged joint's threshold, stood a twelve- to fifteen-foot-long, well-used, marble-topped mahogany bar. The unpretentious back bar was stocked with a modest array of colorfully labeled liquors displayed in shelved, individual assortments that were separated by a large, crystal-clear beveled mirror. Surprisingly, the piece of flawless, reflective glass appeared devoid of cracks or bullet holes applied by gunfire from promiscuous, drunken cowboys or angry losers at the once-busy gaming tables.

A polished brass foot rail the size of a grown man's arm ran around the entire base of the bar and protected four spittoons planted in strategic spots for the use of any customer who might indulge in the tobacco-chewing habit. An inactive potbellied stove occupied the corner at the far end of the bar. Behind the dormant heater stood an exit that opened into the alleyway between the saloon and the nearby Chinese laundry.

At the near end of the marble-topped bar, within arm's reach of a basketlike dice cage, stood a red-faced, sweating, mustachioed drink slinger. He sported a worn but serviceable wine red silk vest and bright red garters on the sleeves of his white shirt. Poor man appeared rooted to the floor in paralytic fear.

Every square inch of available wall space on that side of the cow country cantina not covered by the mirror—including the back bar and racks of liquor—sported an intriguing variety of pictures of nude women posed in a wide-ranging assortment of fetching, eye-catching positions.

One image, larger than all the others, appeared hung specifically to draw the attention of any brush-popping wrangler or potential gambler who might enter the establishment. Hanging in the center of the back wall, next to the entrance of a private billiards room, Longarm espied a copy of a painting widely known as *The Cowboy's Dream.* Portrayed atop a four-wheeled cart, a diaphanously draped, totally naked brunette was glowingly rendered as being pulled across a dark-clouded, turbulent heaven by magnificent solid white and solid black stallions.

Just inside the saloon's entryway on the left stood an inactive roulette arrangement with an accompanying felt betting layout. A glass case nearly two feet high sat atop the game's unused bet placement area. Inside the case, several grayish black, thick-bodied diamondbacked snakes hissed and rattled as they crawled over a mound of paper money and coins. A sign attached to one end of the cage invited gamblers to TRY YER LUCK FER A $1.00.

Nearby was the ubiquitous but idle favorite of all Western gamblers, the faro arrangement. Five tables, covered in green felt for those who preferred poker, marched in a straight line from the faro operation along the wainscoted wall. Kermit Lasher and Obie sat at the last table. Not one other living soul occupied the place, and a tomblike silence seemed to pervade the entire booze parlor.

In a voice that sounded as though the command came directly from the steps of Heaven, Kermit Lasher roared,

"Come on in, gents. Got nothin' to fear. Assure you this'll be a most congenial sit down—if'n you give it a chance."

Longarm turned to Quincy Bates and whispered, "Sounds like God on High when he opens his mouth, don't he?"

Bates nodded as though mesmerized by what he'd just heard. "Makes ice-cold chicken flesh ripple up and down my spine like waves on a windswept Minnesota lake."

Cocked shotguns at the ready, the pair stepped across the Ice House's threshold at the same time. Longarm darted to the near end of the bar, waved the drink slinger aside, and peeked over to see if anyone might have hidden back there. He nodded, said, "Nothin' here," then resumed his spot at Quincy's side. Once as comfortable as they could make themselves with the situation at hand, Longarm elbowed his partner and the men strode to the back of the room. They drew up a few steps away from Kermit Lasher's table.

While as tall as his son Obie, Kermit Lasher bore not the slightest resemblance to either of his male progeny. Tall and gaunt, a well-cropped white beard and mustache decorated the old man's sun-bronzed face. Shoulder-length hair of the same color dangled from beneath a sweat-stained, fawn-colored Stetson crimped in the popular Montana crease. His clean shirt and vest appeared to have been recently pressed. A pair of silver-mounted Colt pistols at his waist were an exact match for those his daughter favored.

Lasher cast a jaundiced glance at Longarm, then said, "Well, Custis Long, I do declare. Been a spell, ain't it? Last met over in the Glass Mountains, if memory serves."

"Sounds about right, Kermit," Longarm said. "Think you'd taken to runnin' with the Briscoe Gang back in them days. I 'uz just workin' as part of a posse then. You and most of them other boys got away from us."

148

"Yeah, but you killed both the Briscoe brothers single-handedly, as I recall. And then the law caught up with me 'bout a year later. Spent two years over in Huntsville for that little lapse in good judgment."

Longarm nodded. "There've been others."

Lasher stared down at the back of one liver-spotted hand, then picked at something invisible on a dried and cracked knuckle. "True enough. None proven, though. Lotta talk, but no proof. Always a lotta foolish talk where the Lasher family's concerned. We've got blamed for a considerable number of crimes we never committed."

"Well, we'll see how this 'un works out, won't we, Kermit?"

"Suppose you're right, Custis. Why don't you gents have a seat." The elder Lasher motioned to a bottle on the table. "Seems I remember you as a feller who likes rye, Marshal Long. Got a jug of the finest money can purchase in a burg like Devils River. She's just sittin' here waitin' for you to partake. Tough gettin' good liquor in a place that's so far out in the country sunshine it has to be brought in by the wagonload."

He pushed a pair of empty shot glasses across the table, then motioned again for the lawmen to sit, but with more firmness and urgency in his gesticulations this time.

"Go on ahead and sit, Quince," Longarm whispered, "I'll stand over by the wall. Get up against it good 'n tight. Watch our backs."

Quincy jerked a chair away from the table, eased into the well-worn seat, then laid the shotgun across his left arm. When Longarm moved to the wall, the older Lasher glanced at him for a second, frowned, then turned his attention back to the local lawman.

Kermit reached for the bottle, pulled the cork, and held it above the empty glasses. "Can I pour you boys one?"

"Go ahead, Kermit," Longarm said. "Quincy might

149

not care for a nip, but I wouldn't mind takin' a whack at your bottle."

Lasher smiled when the potent liquor overran both the tiny tumblers. "Enjoy," he said, corked the bottle, and placed it on the table near his right hand.

Longarm grabbed the fragrant liquor, sniffed, threw it all back in a single gulp, then slapped the glass back onto the table. "Not bad. Would've preferred some a the Gold Label Maryland variety myself, but this'll do."

Quincy Bates let his drink sit. From behind an eyebrow that arched all the way into his hatband, he said, "We're hearin' rumors that the Clinch brothers have taken a local lady captive, Mr. Lasher. That true?"

Lasher tilted his head, grinned, then winked at Bates. "Sorry to admit it, but yes, the tale you heard is true."

"That bein' the case, I want Bell Harvey turned loose and right by-God quick," Bates snapped.

"Well, now, Marshal Bates, there's the ole horsefly in the buttermilk, so to speak. Ain't a-gonna be no turnin' Miss Harvey loose till you hand my falsely accused, wrongly jailed son Dolphus over to me."

Bates leaned on the table with his free elbow. He jabbed a finger in the old man's face and said, "You can just forget that. Dolphus is the prisoner of Marshal Long here. Your son's looking forward to transfer back to Denver for trial on a charge of murder."

"That's horseshit," Obie growled.

Kermit reached over and placed a hand on his son's arm. "Now, let's maintain our calm here, Obie. I'm absolutely certain these here gents ain't lookin' for a fight."

Longarm's fingernail clicked against the checkered stock of Quincy's short-barreled blaster. "True enough, Kermit. If we can avoid a fight, that's fine. But the Clinch boys are already in trouble for counts of assault, public drunkenness, escape, and now kidnapping. Sooner they turn themselves in, the better. Marshal Bates and I'll see they get a fair trial and immediate execution of whatever verdict a jury can hand down on 'em."

"Now, you see, Marshal Long, that's the problem. Can't get the Clinch boys to turn themselves in because they ain't nowhere around these parts right this very minute. See, way it all shook out, them rosy-cheeked, church-goin' lovers of mankind turned your friend Miss Harvey over to me, then skedaddled outta town faster'n a couple a six-legged jackrabbits. Figure they're halfway to Del Rio by now. Be in Mexico by mornin'. Nothin' but tequila and hot-blooded senoritas for them boys down at the Spider Web Lounge."

A knowing look creaked across Longarm's face and settled around the twin muzzles of his blue-gray eyes. "Ardella. Bell's with Ardella, ain't she?"

Kermit Lasher poured himself a shot from the bottle, downed it in one gulp, then slapped the glass back onto the table. "And only me 'n Obie know exactly where that is. Couldn't be any other way, when you think about it, Long. This here squirrelly fandango turned into a family matter the very second you boys locked Dolphus up like some kinda fuckin' animal. Now, I want my son back, and I want 'im back damned quick. But I'm a fair and patient man. Give you till tomorrow mornin' to make up your minds and get it done."

As though he didn't really want to hear the answer, Quincy Bates said, "And just what in the blue-eyed hell do you figure on doin' with Bell if we refuse?"

The old man glared across the table at Devils River's marshal, leaned forward for emphasis, then barked, "Kill 'er, that's what. Deader'n a rusted pump handle. You don't hand Dolphus over to me by nine o'clock tomorrow mornin', your sweet-assed little blacksmithin' twitch won't live to see noon. Guaran-damn-tee it."

In a voice so low everyone at the table had to turn a concentrated ear his direction to hear it, Longarm said, "You know, Kermit, I could put an end to this dance by just blastin' the hell outta the both of you boys right here, right now. Turn this big popper on the pair of you and there won't be enough of either one of ya left to fill up a dustpan."

Obie slapped the poker table's green felt top with a hand the size of an iron camp skillet and snarled, "You'd damn well die tryin' it, lawdog." His massive paw dropped toward the grips of the Remington pistol jammed behind a double-row cartridge belt that appeared to have every loop filled with a fresh shell.

Quincy Bates brought his double-barreled popper to bear on the moose-sized man. Longarm swung his weapon around on the monster's father. "Could pull both a you sons a bitches up by the roots, easy as pickin' daisies. Ardella'd have to show her face sooner or later and we'd have Bell back."

Kermit Lasher grabbed his impetuous son's wrist and forced the hand back up where everyone could see it. The murderous tension across the table jumped from damn near unbearable to thicker than a Kansan's breakfast molasses in January.

Longarm grinned. "Come on now, Obie, you don't really believe you can best four barrels of buckshot with pistols at no more than five feet. I'd have to reassess my entire opinion of you, my man, 'cause that'd make you dramatically stupider'n you look, and that's sayin' a mouthful."

A nervous grimace etched its way onto Kermit Lasher's flushed face as he labored to keep a grip on his slobbering son's wrist. He held a trembling hand out toward Longarm, then said, "Now wait just a fuckin' minute, Long. Either of you go'n do anything stupid and Ardella's got my personal instructions to make sure the Harvey woman wakes up shoein' horses in Satan's personal stable."

Longarm's grin spread into a wide, toothy smile. "Hell, I believe you when you say that could happen, Kermit. But you and Obie'd still both be deader'n a couple a rotten telegraph poles. You let your idiot son get his hand above that table with a gun in it and I'll splatter his big ass all over the wall behind him. Sure would be a shame to go and mess up the saloon's fancy rendition of *The Cowboy's Dream* with Obie's brains."

Of a sudden the old man slapped Obie Lasher hard enough to loosen a set of store-bought fillings in the brute's teeth.

Obie's gun hand darted up to the palm mark across his reddening cheek, then, like a chastised child, he whined, "Damn, Pap, you didn't have to whack me so hard. Wouldna kilt 'em unless you said I could."

"Sorry, boy, but you know as well as I do that when you go and get an idea in your rock-hard noggin, sometimes ain't nothin' short of bein' hit with an ax handle can get it out."

For a second Longarm thought Obie might burst into tears, but Kermit brought everyone's focus back to the problem at hand when he leveled a knobby, ragged-nailed finger at the deputy U.S. marshal and said, "I want Dolphus right here, tomorrow mornin'. Bring 'im in before nine. Just you and him, Marshal Long. And come unarmed, or I swear you'll regret it. Find out you're heeled and it'll be a sad, blood-soaked case of Katy bar the door. Be on your ass like ugly on an armadillo."

Longarm shot a hot look back at the old man and snapped, "You know, Kermit, this ain't much of a town. We could just search every building, one at a time, till we find the two women. Shouldn't be all that hard a job. Bet we could do the whole dance in two, maybe three hours."

The elder Lasher eyeballed Longarm like a strong-willed child. "Be my guest, Marshal, but trust me when I tell you, it won't do you no good. She's hid in a place where you'll never find 'er."

Longarm shook his head, then said, "We'll see, ole man. We'll see."

As the lawdogs moved to leave, Kermit said, "Wait up fer a second, boys." He bent over and reached under the table. Four barrels of heavy-gauge buckshot immediately swung the elder Lasher's direction. One hand in the air in mock surrender, he came up holding Hamp Bodine's missing leg. He tossed the crude appendage onto the table, then said, "Honas got a case of the Christian forgiveness, you know. Felt like he'd been a bit too harsh with your jailer. Wanted me to make sure the man got his leg back."

Qunicy Bates grabbed the chunk of hand-carved wood, then quickly stepped away. "I'll see he gets it, but if you should run into Honas again, by some wild chance, tell 'im he'd best hope I never come across his sorry ass again in this life. Any man who'd beat a one-legged crip-ple with his own artificial leg don't deserve to walk amongst the livin'. Catch sight of the brutal skunk and I'm gonna punch his ticket for the great beyond first chance I get."

Kermit Lasher reared back in his creaking chair. He glared up at the crimson-faced marshal as though staring into the face of a lunatic. "Man's gotta do what a man's gotta do, Marshal." He zeroed in on Longarm for a mo-ment and snarled, "Remember, you bring so much as a toothpick with you tomorrow mornin' and you're dead on the spot. And nobody 'round here'll ever see the woman again."

A big grin flashed across Obie Lasher's face. "Yeah. What Pap just said. Show up a-packin', federal man, and

154

I'll personally squash you like the stinkin'-assed South Texas tumblebug."

Longarm stopped in the entryway of the Ice House, the batwing doors pressed against his back. He held the shotgun out at arm's length, pointed it at Obie Lasher, then said, "Best get your animal back on his leash, Kermit, or I swear he ain't gonna live much longer."

Chapter 16

Longarm and Quincy Bates backed their way out of the Ice House and onto the boardwalk and thence into the grimy street. Neither man let the saloon's front entrance out of sight until they had made it well past Cobb's Dry Goods Store and were almost in front of the Davis House.

The anxiety and tension of the situation finally began to drain away as the pair strolled up to the entrance of the Matador. Quincy Bates let out what sounded like a long sigh of relief. His shoulders sagged and the tension appeared to drain out of the man. "Damnation," he said, "but I could sure 'nuff use a drink now, Long. Why don't we step into the Matador and down one or two, or maybe a dozen, 'fore we head on over to the jail? Be my pleasure to stand for 'em."

Longarm nodded. "My dear ole pappy always said that the finest kind of liquor's the kind somebody else pays for. Little snort after our edgy dance with Kermit and Obie sounds mighty good to me. Let's do 'er."

The Matador's gregarious bar dog hopped off his corner stool, hustled up to the counter, and wiped at an already squeaky clean spot in front of the two lawmen. "Glad to have both you gents stop by the Matador again. Hell, given the stunning lack of business around town these days, I'm glad to see anybody. What's your pleasure?"

Longarm glanced around the grave-quiet dram shop and noted there was not a single other living soul in evidence. He propped his shotgun against the bar. "So quiet in here I bet you could hear a gnat scratchin' his head," he said, then pointed at a bottle of Gold Label Maryland rye. "Just had a shot of some genuinely marginal liquor down at the Ice House. Feel the need for a beaker of the good stuff."

Quincy nodded. He sat his shotgun next to Longarm's, then laid Hamp Bodine's wooden leg across the end of the bar. "Sounds good to me, by God. Set 'em up and leave the bottle, Herb. You two fellers shake and howdy yesterday, Custis?"

"Nope. Didn't have time. Seems I remember as how you appeared at the door, jumped inside, and went to slappin' Dolphus upside the head 'fore we had a chance to get properly acquainted."

As the bartender poured a pair of man-sized dollops in whiskey tumblers, he held out his free hand and said, "Herb Calloway, Marshal Long. Folks 'round here've pretty much spread all the gossip they could dredge up about you over the past day or so."

Longarm shook the grinning man's hand. "Hope some of it was good, Herb."

Calloway slid the bottle across the bar. "Oh, hell yes. Fact is I ain't heard nothin' bad a'tall. Not a single word."

Longarm saluted the man with his glass. "Well, you are one silver-tongued imp, aren't you, Herb?"

"Nice of you to say so," a grinning Calloway said, then took another swipe at the marble countertop with his rag. Once the spot appeared cleaned to his satisfaction, he turned to Quincy Bates. "Had a lot of stuff up here on my bar over the years, Quince. Whiskey, women, cards, dice, guns of every sort and type, knives, hats, boots, spurs, and one son of a bitch put his dog up on my bar. Bet me the mutt could yodel. Weren't true, a course. Skillet-lickin' biscuit eater's still 'round here somewhere. Even held scorpion races on this here counter once. But hell, I cain't for the life a me remember as how anybody ever brought a wooden leg in and threw 'er up on my bar. Never."

"Belongs to Hamp."

Calloway looked like he'd been slapped. "Figured that, but, damn, Quince, how'd he lose it?"

"It's a long story, Herb. Tell you some other time."

Calloway shook his head, threw the wet towel over his shoulder, and headed back to the stool in the corner. He grabbed up an already open copy of a week-old Austin newspaper and was soon deeply engrossed in its contents.

Longarm lifted his glass and turned to Quincy Bates. "Here's to our friends," he said. "They know the worst about us but refuse to believe it."

"Damn right," Bates said, then downed a deep hit from his drink. He set the glass back on the bar, then leaned against it on crossed arms. "What're we gonna do, Long? I don't think we can take Kermit's threat to kill Bell lightly. But, Lord Almighty, turnin' a skunk like Dolphus loose ain't somethin' I'd care to do one bit. Decision about puttin' him on the street again is strictly up to you, bein' as how he's actually your prisoner and all. I'll completely defer to your judgment on that 'un."

Longarm stared at his own image in the mirror behind the bar. "Gotta figure some way to get a weapon smuggled into the Ice House, Quince. I don't trust ole man Lasher any farther'n I could throw one a them big-footed St. Louis draft horses they use to pull beer wagons around town."

Bates shook his head. "Gonna be a tough nut to crack, for damned sure. Cain't imagine that the Lashers will just sit on their calloused rumps at that table in the Ice House until tomorrow mornin'. If we could get inside once they've vacated the premises, maybe we could plant a pistol somewhere."

Longarm cocked his head to one side, held the glass of amber-colored liquid up, sniffed it, then downed the whole shot. Through gritted teeth he said, "How well do you know the drink wrangler workin' at the Ice House?"

"Not well at all, but he'n Hamp are old drinkin' buddies. Think they've been over to the Davis Mountains a time or two on huntin' trips."

Longarm set his glass on the bar and shoved it aside. "Then I think it's best we get on down to the jail and hash this booger out as best we can."

Bates pitched coins onto the bar, grabbed up his shotgun and Bodine's wayward leg, then followed as Longarm pushed through the batwings and hoofed it for the jailhouse.

Longarm had difficulty containing his surprise at how quickly the crotchety jailor had managed to straighten up the mess the Clinch brothers left behind. Given that the one-legged deputy appeared barely able to hobble more than two or three steps at a time on his makeshift crutch, it amazed Longarm that the previous scene of broken furniture and riotous destruction could barely be detected now. The Beast had taken over the reassembled cot and flopped his hawser-sized tail in recognition when the two lawmen reentered the office.

As Longarm explained his plan to plant a pistol somewhere in the Ice House, a grinning Bodine struggled to attach his fake limb. "Yeah, yeah, I hear you. Soon's I get this contraption strapped into place, gonna sneak on down that way, talk with Benjie Clay. Make sure the gun gets hid, then get myself on back here quick as I can."

"That's not all, not by a long shot," Longarm said. "Tomorrow mornin's gonna come a lot quicker'n any of us think. I'd like to walk in and out of the Ice House and still be in one piece. So, here's what I'd like to propose."

He gathered everyone around Marshal Bates's desk, took a blank piece of paper, and quickly sketched a crude map of the town. Using the pencil stub as a pointer, he said, "Quince, there's a clear view of the saloon's front entrance and the entire westernmost wall from the loft opening of Bell's stable. Want you to sneak down there, get set up with a rifle, and watch my back as I lead Dolphus inside."

"Got the perfect weapon for just such an assignment," Bates said, then reached into his gun rack and pulled out an absolutely pristine Winchester model 1876 hunting rifle. The magnificent weapon sported a twenty-eight-inch octagon barrel, a case-hardened receiver, a checkered grip and forearm, and fancy target sights mounted on the grip behind the hammer.

"Damned nice," Emmit Callahan offered.

For a second Longarm gazed at the long shooter as Quincy Bates turned it over in his hands and held it out for admiring eyes to see. "Well, Emmit, maybe Quince has another one in that rack that's just as impressive. Want you to guard the back. When me'n Quince went sneakin' behind all those buildings on that side of the street, I noticed that there's an abandoned jacal kinda catty-cornered to the place and no more'n a hundred feet from the back entrance of the Ice House."

Bates reached into his weapons cache again and pulled out another rifle that could easily have been taken for the exact double of the model 1876. "Matched set," he said.

"Bought the pair of 'em off'n a poor feller what fell on some hard times."

Callahan ran his fingers over the rifle's checkered forearm. "With a shooter like this 'un, long as I'm livin', Marshal Long, you're as safe as if asleep in your mama's arms. Pick the eye out'n a pismire at a hundred paces with this ole gal. Just might have to put the Intimidator aside for this beauty."

Bodine finally got his recently retrieved leg situated properly, stood, and stamped around the office. "God, I'm glad to be off'n that jumped-up crutch. Have to thank ole Honas for sendin' my leg back next time I see 'im. If'n he lives more'n a few seconds after that happy event!" He slapped his thigh, flashed a moonfaced grin, then said, "Now, what do you want me to do tomorrow, Marshal Long? Come on now, gimme my assignment."

"Shotgun at the ready, you're gonna accompany me and Dolphus from the jail, all the way down this side of the street to a spot in front of Woo's Chinese Laundry. Gonna cuff his hands behind him, and I want you to hold on to his cuffs till I get ready to walk him across the alley to the Ice House. Then I want you to take cover inside Woo's place and make sure no one comes up behind us from anywhere back along the street. All of that make sense, fellers?"

Callahan grunted and nodded.

Bodine said, "Yep, uh huh. Yep. Sounds like a damned fine plan to me, Marshal Long."

"Just one question," Quincy Bates said. "Why're we goin' to so much trouble? Why don't we just all march 'im down there, make sure you and Bell come away clean, and then blast the hell out of 'em when they try to leave?"

Longarm scratched a stubble-covered chin. "'Cause I

ain't sure the Clinch brothers have left town the way Kermit claims. Crazy sons a bitches could be hidin' anywhere just waitin' for a chance to kill us all from ambush."

Mad Dog Callahan's eyes lit up. "You really think they're still skulkin' around somewheres, Long?"

"No way to know for sure. But I don't trust Kermit Lasher any farther'n I can throw Obie."

Everyone mumbled his agreement with Longarm's assessment, then he said, "Well, you need to get over to the Ice House quick as you can, Hamp. Probably a good idea for you to take your shotgun and do a tour around town every few hours, Quince. Armed presence on the street should keep the Lasher bunch on their toes. Think it best for you to man the jail while Hamp's out, Emmit."

Bates grabbed his shotgun and headed for the street. "Might as well show a little force right now." He stopped in the open door and said, "What're you gonna do, Custis?"

"Head for my room at Davis House. Have me a bath and shave. Try'n get a couple a hours' sleep 'fore the big dance tomorrow. Be back 'round sunup. If'n you need me, send somebody, and I'll come runnin'. Otherwise make sure you really can't do without my help, 'cause I'd like to put my head on a pillow for a spell, boys."

Mad Dog Emmit waved the remark aside with, "We can take care a everything till mornin', Marshal Long. No need to concern yourself."

Longarm hoofed it for the hotel while Marshal Bates took his time moving from one storefront to the next. Bates rattled doors, spoke to anyone who passed, and generally put on quite a show of making his presence known all over the street.

Longarm marched into Davis House like a man on a mission. He'd barely hit the stairway to the second floor when the persnickety desk clerk popped up and made a hissing, snakelike sound at him. With his hand on the newel post, Longarm turned to see Horace Boykin make vigorous gestures for him to come over.

"Yes? What is it?" Longarm said as he strolled up to the clearly agitated gent.

Shielding his mouth with one hand, Boykin motioned Longarm closer, then whispered, "There's a woman waiting for you upstairs in the hallway, sir."

Longarm leaned back, cast a glance at the second-floor landing, then said, "How do you know she's waiting for me? She tell you that?"

The hotel's desk attendant shook his head. His sand-colored mustache twitched. "Of course not. She marched right in here, asked what room you were in, then stormed upstairs when I told her. Of course I followed her up, then watched as she pulled a chair to a spot next to your door and took a seat. Very forcefully informed her you weren't in there. Well, she pulled a fancy, silver-plated pistol, waved it in my face, and told me to scat. She hasn't moved for at least half an hour."

"Tall, rangy, and blond? Probably carryin' a fancy silver-handled quirt?"

"That's her alright. Heavily armed, too. Had more pistols and knives hangin' off her than any female I've ever met. Hate to have that woman get mad at me, I'll tell you for sure, Marshal Long."

"Well, don't worry 'bout her, Horace. Get me a tub of water ready. I'll send down for it when I'm ready."

Longarm took the stairs two at a time. He spotted the empty, cane-bottomed chair still sitting outside his room as soon as he turned into the hallway. With the Frontier model Colt in hand, he slipped up to the partially open door. From inside he heard, "Come on in, Marshal Long. It's safe."

He stepped into the room to find Ardella Lasher, hands

164

raised in surrender, sitting in a chair she'd dragged in from the balcony. Her double-holstered pistol rig, backup gun, and bowie knife all dangled from the knobbed post at the foot of the bed. She had unbuttoned her brocade vest, removed the cowboy cuffs, and kicked off her fancy stitched boots.

"I'm not armed, Marshal. Hope you don't mind, but it's a mite more comfortable in here. Nicer chairs," she said, then flashed a saucy grin.

Chapter 17

Longarm glanced into every shadowy corner of the room before he holstered the big Colt and said, "What the hell you doin' here, Ardella?"

The girl stood, then barefooted her way to within arms's reach. She appeared truly repentant when she cooed, "Just wanted to let you know I don't approve of Pap's tactics, takin' Bell Harvey and all, and that I've decided to get away from this mess."

"Ah. And exactly what does 'get away' mean?"

She tilted her head like a curious puppy. "Well, me and Pap have had our differences of opinion about more'n a few things in the past, to the point where I've threatened to leave him to his depravities on more than one occasion prior to this dance. Just decided I wouldn't be a party to his brutal methods this time around."

"That a fact? Thought from the way you chomped on us yesterday down at the jail, you had no problem whatsoever with anything your dear ole daddy wanted to do to get your idiot brother Dolphus loose."

She snaked an arm out, ran a finger under Longarm's shirt, and tickled a spot on his chest. "Well, if he had decided to face you head-on, I might've been right there

167

beside him. Might've been forced to shoot you myself. But I don't like the idea of usin' an innocent, kidnapped woman as a pawn in a game as deadly as this one. Pap's never done anything like this before, and I, for one, won't have any part of it. Told him so, too. He blessed me out and told me I could get on back to our place over on Elephant Mountain. Not sure that's where I'm headed, but I'm gettin' out before the killin' starts."

"Didn't come by my room just to keep me occupied while Kermit, Obie, and the Clinch boys try to pull something nefarious, did you?"

She took another step and pushed a set of proud young breasts and thumb-sized, bullet-hard nipples up against his chest, then squirmed from side to side. The tips of her knockers were so stiff he could feel them all the way through his vest and shirt. Her hand came up between Longarm's legs and persistent fingers curved around the treasure they found.

The wickedly playful girl flashed an impish smile as she gave the awakening giant behind the crotch of his brown tweed pants a vigorous rubbing. She stood so close he could detect the lingering aroma of a lilac-scented soap in her free-swinging blond hair.

When the brazen female squeezed his aroused dingus and then began to jerk on it, Longarm sucked in a ragged breath and grabbed her by the shoulders. "You absolutely sure Kermit didn't send you over here, Ardella?"

"Abso-fuckin'-lutely. Came on my own, by God. Been thinkin' 'bout you, and whatever I've got hold of here, ever since we met down in the jailhouse. If Pap was to find out 'bout what I'm doin', he'd likely whip me like a yard dog."

Longarm ran his hands up under the panting girl's breasts, gathered a double handful, squeezed, then pinched her nipples. She snatched her muslin shirt open and set the big puppies loose to play.

As the shirt and vest floated to the floor like wounded doves, Ardella's hands slid up beneath her firm, heavy breasts and pushed them toward her waiting tongue. She licked a nipple until it appeared to have achieved a level of steely hardness similar to that of a rifle barrel. She sucked on it, then switched to its neglected mate. Dark, thick areolas as big around as a silver dollar thickened and raised the erect, inflamed nipples even farther.

"Ole Kermit still whips you, darlin'?"

The girl's greedy mouth came away from her nipple with a wet, juicy *pop*. She continued to massage her boobs as she said, "He's even been known to take a switch to Obie on occasion. Don't have any problem whippin' my behind once in a while, for damned sure."

Longarm pitched his hat onto the room's chest of drawers, then closed the door with one foot. He stripped his pistol belt off and tossed the weapon onto a chair beside the bed. Jacket, vest, and shirt followed. Before making a move toward the girl, he grabbed up his gun leather and weapon and draped the rig over the headboard just in case the lady was in the process of leading him down the primrose path to destruction.

Once prepared for any unseen eventuality, he dipped two fingers into Ardella's luscious nookie and at the same time thumbed the buttons loose on his pants. The amazingly long, downy hair around her glory hole felt like a gooey nest of silken threads. The girl gasped, grabbed his hand, hunched against the invading fingers several times, then let out a mewling, barely audible squeak.

"God Almighty," she wheezed. "We just started and you've already made me cream all over myself. Been quite a spell since any man's had this kind of effect on me, Long. Gonna have me drippin' all over the floor soon." With no warning whatsoever, she dove at his crotch and soon had most of him in her greedy mouth.

Took some doing, but after a matter of less than a minute Longarm had managed to get himself and the anxious, randy girl completely naked. Most of that time he had to fight like a wildcat to keep her away from his harder-'n-a-pick-handle prong. Seemed that the more he worked at getting her bare-assed, the more vigorously she worked at trying to keep his cock lodged against the back of her throat. The skintight leather riding skirt proved so problematic, he was forced to push her back in order to strip the garment away.

"Oh, jeez," she moaned, then grabbed him again and ran the tip of her tongue around the blood-engorged head of his throbbing doinker.

Eventually the heat and urgency shooting off the girl locked a carnal grip around his ability to control himself. He grabbed Ardella Lasher under the arms, raised her off the floor, and pitched her onto the bed. She bounced, squealed, giggled, and then raised her shapely ass as high as possible off the mattress.

One of the flushed gal's hands darted into her dewy, down-covered snatch and, as she gave herself a vigorous, clawing hand job, she moaned, "Come and get it, Long. Shove that big ole thang up in here and bang me till I speak in heathen tongues not heard since biblical times. Good God, I've been thinkin' 'bout this for hours."

Longarm climbed onto the bed and moved up between her waiting legs. She wrapped herself around him, snapped her heels together, then grabbed his dingus and greedily guided it into the glorious waiting warmth of her already juicy, squirting cooz. Her writhing body rose to meet his every athletic stroke. He quickly realized there was no real need to slowly plumb the depths of her sex before getting up to speed. Ardella Lasher had a man in the saddle and was more than ready for a serious humping.

Longarm used his stringy-muscled, pile-driving ass to

drill into her bucking, snorting body with all the enthusiasm of a hoedown fiddler with a hot bow. Their taut, sweat-dripping bellies made loud, nasty slapping sounds as they crashed against each other. The thrashing girl threw her arms around his neck and pulled him down as though she wanted their bodies merged together in a single, quivering, spurting fountain of lust.

Prepared to make a leisurely, enjoyable run at the situation, Longarm soon realized that the energetic Ardella would have none of his ill-conceived plans. Her hips were a blur of action as she brought her belly up against his, then ground her steaming, juicy crotch against him with a fiery doggedness he'd rarely encountered. She lifted her shaggy head, and when their lips ground together he thought she might well suck the tongue right out of his mouth. The heat of her efforts soon had him on the very edge of explosive climax.

Sensing the urgency of his need, Ardella quickened the pistonlike motion of her hips. She grabbed his head, then tongued his ear till he thought he might loose consciousness.

In one final, plunging lunge, Longarm pinned the thrashing girl's athletic ass to the bed. His spine drawn as tight as a banjo string, he emptied himself into Ardella's lava-hot, squirting quim. After a full minute of extended pressure to maintain his final thrust, Longarm gently let himself down and rolled to one side.

Just before his tired eyes closed in exhaustion, he heard Ardella Lasher whisper in his ear, "Don't trust Pap, darlin'. He'll kill you if he can. And if he doesn't, Obie will."

He had the Colt out of its oiled holster before his eyes had fully opened. Unsure of exactly what jarred him awake, Longarm sat bolt upright in the bed and tried to penetrate the room's hazy darkness with uncooperative eyes. He ran a hand to his forehead, then ruffed his sweat-dampened hair.

A barely audible tap at the door was followed by, "Your bath is ready, Marshal. Shall we bring it in?"

He felt around the bed. Empty. Ardella had somehow managed to get dressed and sneak out without waking him. Surprised by the realization, he hopped out of the bed, covered himself with a convenient pillow, and tip-toed over to the door. Standing to one side, he called out, "That you, Boykin?"

From the hallway, the Davis House's prickly desk clerk replied, "Indeed, sir. The very one. Saw the lady take her leave. When you didn't send down for me, thought it best to come on up, as you seemed so resolute about the bath earlier."

Longarm cracked the door open, then eyeballed his tormentor. "You alone, Boykin?"

An exasperated look of near total frustration darted across the clerk's face, then he said, "Just me and my stalwart helper, Jose Delgado. Can't get your bath up these fucking stairs by myself, sir."

"What time is it?"

"A few minutes after ten, sir. Do you still wish to bathe?"

Longarm stood to one side, snatched the door open, and watched the men lug the wooden tub in, then tote in ten buckets of water two at a time until the tub was filled. Still naked as a jaybird and covering himself with the pillow, he fumbled through his trouser pockets for change, then tipped both men handsomely for their efforts as they left. He slammed the door shut, threw the pillow back onto the bed, and stepped into the waiting tub of sparkling well water.

Thirty minutes later, Longarm dropped onto his bed, clean, refreshed, and, thank God, even a bit cooler. It was

172

then he noticed the note attached to the end of his pillow. In a rough hand that looked more like something written by an illiterate brush popper, Ardella Lasher had scribbled, "Memmember what I sayed afore you crapped out on me, Big Boy. Kermit wil kil you dade if'n he gits a chanst. If'n not him, the Obie wil do fer you. Be keerful. I'm headed fer Elephant Mountain."

Before he dropped off to sleep, Longarm fished the watch from his vest pocket and made a mental note to wake up at 4:00 A.M. sharp the next morning. Through years of practice, he had developed the uncanny ability to trick himself into arising at precise times even though he had no access to an alarm clock. His convenient skill proved especially handy when on the trail, but worked just as well in town. He checked the loads in the twin-barreled .44-caliber derringer attached to the other end of his gold watch chain, snapped the tiny pistol closed, then drifted off to sleep.

At exactly 4:15 the following morning, Longarm's eyes popped open as though hinged to his skull like paper window shades on spring rollers. Although the drowsy lawman was in no hurry, in less than an hour he had dressed, checked the loads of his various weapons, strapped the Frontier model Colt around his waist, then thumped his way down Davis House's stairs and into the street.

In spite of understanding that a town of Devils River's size wouldn't normally have much, if any, foot traffic at such an hour, the normal stillness of the fading burg's main thoroughfare struck Longarm as somehow slightly eerie and a bit unsettling. He sauntered to a stop beside a porch pillar in front of Maynard's Drug Store, two doors down from the Matador, then slipped a cheroot from his inside jacket pocket. A slow, studied examination of the entire street, from one end to the other, took place before

173

he scratched a match to life on a porch pillar. He flicked the dead, still-smoking lucifer into the dirt, then hot-footed his way across the street when he noticed flickering lamplight in one of the jailhouse's side windows.

Calloused knuckles gently applied to Marshal Quincy Bates's front door brought an immediate response from inside. "Who the hell's out there? Best identify yerself, or get blasted to kingdom come sure as chickens have feathers."

"Open the door, Emmit. It's me, Longarm," he hissed through the thick set of iron-bound plank panels.

The bolt slid away and the uneasy lawman eased inside, pushed the door closed, and secured the entrance behind him. A darting glance around the dimly lit room revealed his three bleary-eyed confederates in various states of dress, undress, and armament. He headed for the coffeepot and poured into a tin cup some of Hamp Bodine's up-an'-at-'em juice that looked strong enough to float one of those old Colt Walker pistols. The other men continued to get clothed while he sipped at his steaming rasher of stump juice.

Bodine buttoned his shirt and grinned as though waiting for a compliment on his coffee-cooking ability, but Longarm ignored the obvious hankering for praise and snapped, "Your friend get me a weapon hid somewhere handy, Hamp?"

The feisty jailer seemed somewhat taken aback, but nodded.

Quincy Bates jumped in as he pulled his pants up and said, "Not more'n an hour ago, Hamp snuck down to the Ice House alone, Custis. Got inside and nailed a holster to the underside of the first table on the left past the roulette setup and snake box when you enter the place. Pistol's a Frontier model .45, just like that 'un you carry. Has a hot load in every chamber."

Bodine recovered, gave a vigorous nod of the head, then added, "Gun's situated for whoever takes a seat at the very first chair you have to pass on enterin' the place. Fitted the holster so you can sit ole Dolphus on your left or right, whichever's most convenient. That way you'll have a seat facin' the back of the room for yourself and be able reach under the table and get armed up. Spot also puts the roulette wheel, the faro operation, and them damned snakes 'tween you and the front door."

Longarm blew over the cup of steaming liquid, then said, "Sounds good, but why the front table? You could have picked the second or third one just as easy."

Bodine bobbed his head and grinned. "Well, I figured Lasher'd have the woman in the corner at the back of the room, as far away from the batwings as he could get 'er. Thought maybe ole Kermit would probably wanna start the two prisoners walkin' toward each other so's they'd just pass one another in the space 'tween the bar and the poker tables."

Longarm nodded. Took another sip from the dense liquid, then said, "Damn. All sounds mighty good, Hamp, but I think I might need something in the way of a backup just in case Kermit, or maybe even that idiot Obie, don't hold to doin' what we expect."

"Thought a that possibility, too, Marshal Long," Bodine said with a big smile. "Emptied the spittoon at the bar, directly across from that first table. Even moved it from behind the foot rail. Put 'er out front. Cain't miss the one I'm talkin' 'bout. Dropped a short-barreled .38-caliber Lightning down inside. Fit perfect. All you gotta do is reach in, pull 'er out, and start blazin' away. Know she ain't as powerful as that big ole .45, but she's better'n nothin' and only there in case everthang else goes to hell on a bobsled and you absolutely need it."

For the first time that morning, Longarm allowed himself a slight smile. "Well thought out, Hamp. You did a fine job."

Bodine beamed with real pride.

"Yeah," Quincy added, "and he didn't have to do anything to involve the bartender. This way we're the only ones who have any knowledge of the planted weapons."

Longarm nodded. "Grand, just grand. Reckon you and Emmit best get started toward your posts, Quincy. Want you boys all set up and ready for this dance long before Kermit and Obie even wake up."

Finally dressed and ready to go, Callahan and Quincy grabbed a variety of weapons, including the Winchesters, and headed for the door. Callahan carried the flashy Intimidator in one hand, a rifle in the other.

Longarm held up a hand just as Quincy's fingers gripped the front door's knob. "I should get to the Ice House's swingin' doors at exactly nine o'clock by my watch," he said and patted the pocket of his vest. "Gonna have to lay around in your hidey-holes for a couple a hours. So try not to go to sleep. Don't want anyone coming in behind me, or sneaking in from the back of the place once I get inside that nest a vipers. Oh, and one other thing. If either of you see me come out of the Ice House at a run, with Bell Harvey in tow, get ready to start killin' people, 'cause there's a good chance someone's gonna be hot on our heels. You boys stay sharp, and maybe we'll all come outta this mess alive and unharmed."

Mad Dog Callahan shook his Winchester in the air like a painted Comanche. "Damned right," he growled.

Bates slapped his enormous friend on the shoulder and pushed him over the threshold and into the hazy approach of dawn.

Chapter 18

"Well, I see by my official Ingersoll railroader's pocket watch that it's now exactly eight thirty," Longarm said. He rose from one of the less-than-comfortable cane-bottomed chairs next to Quincy Bates's chess setup, blew a smoke ring the size of a galvanized washtub toward the jail's open-beamed ceiling, and snapped the case of his fancy ticker closed. Well-chewed cheroot firmly clasped between pearly choppers, the still-drowsy-eyed deputy marshal turned to Hamp Bodine, then said, "Time to bring 'im out."

Bodine eagerly pulled himself from the cushioned comfort of Quincy Bates's favorite seat, hobbled over to the cell block door, and snatched it open. Through the gaping opening he yelled, "Git yer sorry ass off'n my cot, you shit-eatin' son of a bitch. We're about to take us a little stroll."

As Longarm pinched the bridge of his nose and rested tired eyes, he heard Bodine thump his way back to the farthest cell, key the heavy lock, and swing the barred gate aside.

Sporting sprigs of straw from the jailhouse mattress, and still decorated with spotty patches of crusted blood along the stitched gash on the side of his head, Dolphus Lasher stumbled into the office and blinked his rheumy eyes. "Sure could use me a big ole cup a hot coffee." He pointed at the pot and made a gimme motion with a trembling finger.

From his spot atop the reconstituted cot, the Beast growled and snapped its enormous jaws together. Lasher hopped to one side and glared down at the animal.

"Right scary, ain't he?" Bodine said, and pushed Lasher closer to a spot near the gun rack.

Longarm strode across the room. A pair of iron manacles dangled from one hand. He grabbed Lasher by the arm and snapped a cuff around the surprised killer's wrist. Then he jerked both the struggling man's limbs behind him and shackled the second arm to the first.

Lasher glared over his shoulder at Longarm. "What the hell's this all about? Bad 'nuff I cain't get no sleep in this dump. Seems like ever' time I turn around, you sons a bitches is draggin' me outta my cell and treatin' me like some kinda animal. Don't have to put me in irons. Ain't gonna try an' get away. Figure you bastards would most likely shoot me in the back just fer the fun of it, if'n I did."

Longarm pushed the mouthy outlaw across the room and forced him to sit in one of the chess table's empty chairs. As he moved around to a spot where he could face Lasher, he smacked the outlaw on the back of the head. The sharply delivered lick knocked the brigand's head forward, but with some quick thinking the evil skunk managed to keep his hat from falling off.

Invigorated by the application of a wee bit of personal vengeance, Longarm took a seat on a corner of the rough table and said, "Listen up. We're gonna take a little midmornin' stroll down to the Ice House. Yer dear ole daddy's worked a trade. We're gonna swap your sorry, murderin' ass for the lady who owns the town's black-smith and stable operation."

Of a sudden, Lasher's entire demeanor changed. His spine straightened. He drew his shoulders back, poked his narrow chest out, and threw a defiant, teeth-gritting gaze up at Longarm. "I knew Pap wouldn't let you take me to Denver to get my neck stretched. Man would surely die if'n I wuz ever forced to mess myself in front of a buncha drunk yahoos what come to see me die. Tell you right now, Long, you're one damned lucky cocksucker if'n he don't kill the hell outta you 'fore this is all over."

Longarm leaned down to where his nose almost touched Lasher's. "Listen to me, you stupid son of a bitch. You, me, and Hamp are gonna take a slow stroll down the street from here to the Ice House. Durin' that little ramble, you're gonna keep that slit trench you call a mouth closed."

Lasher let out a derisive snicker, then said, "Aw, fuck you, you law-pushin' asshole. Talk anytime I damn well please."

Longarm's open palm almost knocked the smart-mouthed murderer out of his seat. A second, more vigor-ously delivered slap caused Lasher's hat to fly off. The fancy sombrero landed on the table and knocked most of the chess pieces over.

"Say one word to me after we walk out the jailhouse door, Dolphus, and I'll bust you 'cross the nose with my pistol barrel. Put you down like a poleaxed horse. Then, I swear 'fore bleedin' Jesus, I'll drag your sorry behind through the dirt the rest of the way to the Ice House—no matter how far that turns out to be."

Red-faced and shaking, Lasher muttered, "Didn't have to fuckin' slap me, you son of a bitch."

The stern-faced deputy U.S. marshal smacked Lasher

again, then shook a finger in the surprised murderer's face. "I ain't playin' with you, Dolphus. You rabbit on me and I'll let Hamp drop you with a load a buckshot between the shoulder blades 'fore you've gone two steps. Obie or the Clinch boys pop out of an alley, fall off a roof at our feet, or storm past on horses shootin' as they go by, and he's got my permission to blow you outta your boots. Your pap tries to pull anything shady, you'll end up the deadest man in Texas times three. Got any questions?"

A trickle of blood ran from the corner of his mouth as Lasher shook his head.

Longarm stuffed the chastised miscreant's hat back on his head, then jerked him to his feet. He stripped off his own jacket and vest, then tossed them onto Marshal Bates's desk. He lifted and resettled his pistol belt, then glanced over at a smiling Hamp Bodine and said, "You screwed down and sittin' deep, Deputy Bodine? Ready for this ride to start?"

Bodine brought his shotgun up and propped it against his hip. "Got my leg strapped on tight and both barrels cocked. Turn 'er loose and let 'er buck, Marshal Long."

Longarm led the way into the street. He pointed out a spot behind Lasher where he wanted Bodine, then shoved Dolphus toward the boardwalk on the far side of the street. The trio mounted the raised walkway in front of Godwin's Meat Market and turned west.

Over his shoulder, Longarm said, "Keep an eye open on the windows and the roof line across the street, Hamp. I'll watch the doorways and the thoroughfare ahead. Got that?"

Bodine grunted as he limped along on his recently recovered leg and said, "You're covered, Marshal Long. You're covered."

Though not much more than a hundred yards, the walk

seemed interminable to Longarm. By the time they finally reached the corner of Woo's Chinese Laundry, he had developed a belly full of bedsprings and was well on the way to acquiring a crick in his neck from looking over his shoulder.

Sweat poured from under his arms and saturated a strip up his back, when Longarm touched Dolphus on the arm and said, "Hold up." He unbuckled his pistol belt, handed the entire rig to Bodine, then raised his arms and turned around in a circle. "You see anything that looks like a weapon on me, Hamp?"

Bodine cocked his head to one side like an old dog in the process of deciding whether to scratch at a flea in its ear. "Tight as them pants are, Longarm, I don't think you could hide much a anythang under 'em."

Longarm snorted, pushed Dolphus toward the Ice House, then waved at Bodine as he followed. He grabbed his prisoner by the short piece of chain between the cuffs just before they made it to the batwing doors. While holding the younger Lasher in check, he called out, "Got your son out here, Kermit."

From deep inside the saloon he heard the boy's father yell, "Well, come on in, goddammit. 'S why yer here, for Christ's sake."

Longarm grabbed Dolphus by the arm and hissed, "When we get to the first table on your left, I want you to go to the chair nearest the wall and have a seat. Don't say a word, don't move, don't even breathe unless I tell you to. Got all that?" From behind a curled-lipped sneer, Lasher nodded. Then Longarm pushed him though the door and followed.

Soon as they pulled up even with the first poker table, Dolphus headed for his assigned seat and insolently flopped into it. Longarm sat down in the chair nearest the faro layout, felt for the hideout pistol, and immediately found it exactly according to Bodine's description. Good man, he thought, then leaned back in the chair and brought his left hand up to his chin.

After fifteen seconds or so, Longarm's eyes had finally grown accustomed to the dimly lit interior of the dram shop. Of a sudden he realized that something didn't feel right, didn't sound exactly right, but he couldn't quite put a finger on where the problem lay. There was definitely something out of place. That's when he noticed Bell Harvey. For a second he felt as though Obie Lasher had punched him in the gut.

Kermit and Obie sat at the same table they'd occupied the last time they'd all met. But Bell was tied to the pot-bellied stove in the corner at the end of the bar. Atop the stove sat the case full of rattlers that normally decorated the unused roulette table he'd passed when he and Dolphus entered the room. Bell's back was pressed against the glass case, and she twisted at her bindings and looked mighty uncomfortable, but otherwise she seemed fine. At least as far as Longarm could tell from near forty feet away.

Kermit said, "Told you to come unarmed, didn't I, Long."

Longarm stood, raised his arms, did a slow pirouette, then dropped back into his seat. "As you can see I ain't got no weapons on me, Kermit. Kept my end of our agreement. Have Dolphus here for the trade. He's safe, sound, and, near as I can tell, don't have a batch of deadly, poisonous snakes strapped to his backside. So I'd thank the hell outta you boys if one of you'd get off your ass, cut Miss Harvey loose, and see she gets shed of those critters."

Kermit Lasher came out of his chair as though his lanky old ass had a coil of steel spring attached. He shook

182

a knotted finger at Longarm and thundered, "You ain't in no position to make any kinda goddamned demands, you star-struttin' asshole. Now take them cuffs off'n my boy 'fore I come over there, kill you, then let Obie do fer the girl." Then Lasher reared back, fisted hands on his hips and, as though proud to say it, added, "'Course, knowin' my oldest son the way I do, would imagine he'd prefer to fuck the hell out a this here gal first."

Grinning like a certifiable idiot who'd finally been given permission for an unspeakable act, Obie Lasher drunkenly lurched to unsteady feet, then staggered toward Bell Harvey. The panic-stricken woman screamed into the gag over her mouth and struggled with the ropes binding her to the stove.

Obie took two whiskey-fueled steps, stumbled, and crashed headfirst into the glass case filled with snakes. He wobbled to his feet with the fractured cage hanging around his neck like a demented picture frame. A monstrous rattler squirmed in each hand. Another of the writhing creatures dangled from one of his cheeks, and still a third was attached to an uncovered place on his neck near the man's jugular vein. He whirled around to reveal still more of the hideous creatures hanging from points all over his back. The TRY YER LUCK FER A $1.00 sign had also attached itself to Obie, dangled from the gyrating man's waist, and covered his crotch at a bizarre angle. The entire demented scene struck Longarm as something out of a lunatic's nightmare.

Stunned by the astonishing developments, Longarm grabbed the pistol from the holster attached to the underside of the table and held it in his lap. He flashed the weapon at Dolphus and motioned for him not to move. At that exact instant Obie Lasher let out a screech that people in Del Rio could have heard over a thunderstorm of the type that only occurs once every five hundred years.

Then, to everyone's total amazement, Dolphus's mountainous, bug-eyed, purple-faced brother started running for the Ice House's batwings. He reeled into tables and knocked chairs over. Snakes flew off the man in every direction. Longarm ducked as the distraught man wobbled past, squealing like a lunch whistle at a sawmill. The horrified Obie hit the swinging doors so hard one flew off its hinges, but he couldn't have made it much past the boardwalk when gunshots rang out and his terrified screeching abruptly stopped.

Pistol in hand, Longarm rose from his seat. He reached over and snatched Dolphus to his feet. "Jig's up, Kermit."

An unhinged look spread over the elder Lasher's face as he came up with a pistol in each hand. A thunderous blast from one weapon chewed a fiery hole within inches of Longarm's right ear. The old man's poorly aimed second shot scorched a six-inch path in the top of the table in front of the lawman's prisoner, ricocheted off, then hit the surprised killer dead center.

Unable to cover the thumb-sized hole that spewed a foot-long geyser of hot blood from his chest, Dolphus pulled himself loose from his captor's grip and stumbled toward his stunned father. The dying brigand's life sprayed onto the wall and spattered every stick of furniture in his path.

Within steps of Kermit's table, Dolphus stopped, swayed like a willow in a windstorm, then gaped at the hole in his chest and said, "Damn, Pap. What'd you do?" He fell forward, hit the tabletop with his dead face, then rolled onto the floor in a motionless heap.

For a second the only sounds in the saloon were the buzz of the snakes' rattlers, Bell's muffled screams, and Kermit Lasher's strained breathing. Then a series of thunderous shots rang out from behind the saloon. Lasher cast a bug-eyed glare at the saloon's rear exit. He threw his head back and let out a shriek that sent gooseflesh up Longarm's back. Both men raised their pistol-filled hands at the same instant.

Custis Long's only shot hit the old man an inch above his right eye. The 255-grain slug punched a hole in Kermit Lasher's skull, then sliced through his fevered brain like a heated ice pick shoved through a cannonball-sized gob of butter. The back of Lasher's head exploded in a glob of blood, bone, and hair that splattered the watering hole's fancy painting of *The Cowboy's Dream*. The old man's unblinking corpse dropped to the floor like an empty shuck.

Longarm jumped to the spittoon near the bar's foot rail, grabbed the second hidden pistol, then strode toward Bell Harvey. He kicked snakes out the way and blasted several to pieces as he went. Upon arrival at her side, he quieted the horrified girl by raising the barrel of the Frontier model Colt like a shushing finger.

"Think Obie took most of 'em slimy sons a bitches with him when he left, Bell. I've killed those I could see. Don't hear any more of 'em buzzin'. Now, I'm gonna lay my pistols on the stovetop, get my pocketknife out, and cut you loose. Want you to be as calm as possible. Understand?"

Although wild-eyed and shaking like the last leaf on a lightning-struck oak, Bell groaned, then nodded. Longarm took his time, cut her loose, retrieved his weapons, then said, "Carefully, now. Follow me. Try to step where I've already stepped. I'll get you outta here."

Once on the boardwalk, Bell Harvey fell onto Longarm's chest like an exhausted swimmer saved from drowning. "God," she said, "thought you'd never come."

He shoved the pistols into the waistband of his pants, placed one hand on her cheek, then said, "They hurt you, darlin'?"

She shook her head. "No. The old man made sure of that. Said they couldn't touch me or do anything until Dolphus was free, or you were good'n dead. Think Obie overreacted when he hopped up and started my direction."

Longarm glanced into the street. No more than thirty feet from the saloon's front entrance, Quincy Bates stood with his Winchester propped against one hip as he toed at the oozing corpse of Obie Lasher.

As Longarm led Bell into the street, Emmit Callahan strode around the corner. He hooked a thumb toward the back of the Ice House. "Clinch brothers is back yonder. Got 'em both. They 'uz hidin' out in a little grove a trees 'tween here and the river. Came a-runnin' soon's they heard the first shots from inside the Ice House. Hell, it 'uz just like shootin' ducks. Intimidator cut 'em down like a scythe through dry wheat."

Hamp Bodine hobbled over. Man had tears rolling down his cheeks.

"Find your bartender friend's body, Hamp?" Longarm said.

Bodine stared at his only remaining foot. "Poor man's stuffed in a barrel back there in the alley 'tween the saloon and Woo's. Looks to me like he's been dead since last night. Probably explains why I 'uz able to get inside the place and hide them guns so easy."

Color came up in Bell Harvey's face. She grabbed Longarm's hand and pulled him toward her stable and smith operation. When they'd got out of earshot of the other men, she said, "Can't explain it, but there's just something 'bout gunfire and bloody death that makes me wanna do the big wiggle till I'm too tired to flop."

In spite of himself, Longarm grinned. "Know what you mean. And I'm just the man to help you with that particular overwhelmin' feelin'."

Bell looped her arm over his. "Have a bedroom up in

the loft, Custis. Stay there nights when I can't get home. Gonna take you upstairs and thank you for savin' me till you're so raw you'll have to walk bowlegged for the next two months."

Longarm threw his head back and chuckled, then said, "Well, darlin', try not to hurt me too bad. Could be somethin' of a problem if your lovin' forced me to tell my superiors I'd been crippled by a grateful woman."

Watch for

**LONGARM AND THE
CROOKED MADAM**

the 362nd novel in the exciting LONGARM
series from Jove

Coming in January!